"You can't run away from love forever, Alex."

Marg placed a hand on hers. "Sooner or later it's going to sneak up on you, and you need to be ready."

Alex didn't draw her hand away, as was her first inclination. She didn't want to hurt her mother's feelings.

"Mother, I'm perfectly happy with my life. I'm not interested in long-term."

"You see, that's my point. You should be," Marg countered. "You think I couldn't get a job. You think I couldn't get a place if I didn't have this one. Well, you're wrong. I could make it on my own. I might fall down now and then, but there's nothing wrong with that."

Alex wasn't sure where she was going with all this.

"It's okay to fail every so often. Life isn't supposed to be perfect. Living life is about taking risks, about allowing yourself to be vulnerable at times," Marg insisted. "You *need* to fall. Otherwise you're never going to know just how magical life is."

Debra Webb

Debra Webb's romantic-suspense publishing career was launched with her first Harlequin Intrigue novel in September 2000. Since then this award-winning, bestselling author has had more than fifty novels hit the shelves. She spends most of her research in one of three ways—picking the brain of any FBI agent who will listen, following around her favorite local private investigator, or reading about new technology and bizarre criminal cases. Her family and friends have come to expect this sort of behavior and are rarely surprised anymore. Her favorite television shows, *24* and *Grey's Anatomy*, showcase perfectly her love of suspense along with her wicked sense of humor.

never happened

DEBRA WEBB

NEVER HAPPENED

copyright © 2006 by Debra Webb

isbn-13: 9780373880997

isbn-10:   0373880995

TheNextNovel.com

 HARLEQUIN®

PRINTED IN U.S.A.

From the Author

Dear Reader,

Thanks so much for picking up my first Harlequin NEXT novel! I was so excited when asked to write this project. Alex Jackson and her somewhat quirky occupation of cleaning up dead things was a story I definitely wanted to tell.

As a fortysomething myself, I can relate to the career issues as well as the complex romance needs of a woman barreling toward that half-century mark. Reaching forty and then onto fifty is a wonderful and, at times, frustrating time for a woman. I still feel youthful and ambitious and downright sexy. I refuse to allow anyone to make me feel otherwise. In my opinion the greatest thing about being over forty is that I can still be all those things but I have the wisdom necessary for making much better decisions than I did at twenty or even thirty.

So enjoy these years, ladies. Challenge yourself and never, ever let anyone make you feel like anything less than the brilliant, sexy woman you are. Life is full of wonderful surprises and you never know what might happen next!

Cheers,

Debra Webb

This book is dedicated to an editor who challenged me to write the very best book possible. Without her vision and close attention to detail *Never Happened* would not be the fabulous, fun read it is.
Thank you, Jennifer Green, for your dedication to and your passion for the written word.

CHAPTER 1

"You're early, Alex." A wide grin accompanied the remark. "You know I can't let you get started just yet."

The smart-ass cop was right. Charlie Crane's body was still in the house when Alex arrived. She surveyed the scene, could have done without seeing the old guy with his head all mangled by the bullet that had passed through his skull, but there was no changing that stomach-turning fact now.

"Yeah, well, Henson," she said, shifting her gaze from the poor bastard in the easy chair, "you're late. You guys were supposed to be out of here an hour ago."

Detective Rich Henson snorted at her comeback. "The M.E. had a little fender bender, but he'll be here any minute now, and then—" he spread his arms widely to indicate the room "—the place is all yours."

As Henson spoke, his gaze slid down her Margaritaville T-shirt, pausing ever so briefly on her 36D cups, before trailing the length of her jean-clad legs. She'd gotten used to the leers ages ago. Despite being called Alex by all who knew her, she was one hundred percent female and damned proud of it.

Alexis Jackson was thirty-nine—okay, forty, but she wasn't telling anyone since she remained in staunch denial of the fact—five feet six, and one-hundred-ten pounds of well-toned muscle and hard-earned grit and determination. She wore her hair long, straight and blond—her methods for keeping it that way were a closely guarded secret. The men she dated, including the one visually eating her up right now, liked to wax on about how the color of her eyes reminded them of the sea.

Sounded great, huh? Well, the downside to being a blue-eyed blonde with a great body was that most men, and some women, mistakenly thought she was just another pretty face. But they only made that mistake once.

"Who hired you?" Henson asked, being his usual nosy self. Alex felt pretty sure he didn't really care; he just wanted to make conversation. She knew he still had a thing for her, and if she was into long-term relationships and cute guys with adrenaline-driven egos she might just give him a second chance. The fact of the matter was they had been there, done that and she'd walked away.

Besides, cops were off-limits. As were firemen, P.I.'s and paramedics. Give her a CPA anytime. At least she didn't spend all her time stroking his ego. Unfortunately, in her line of work most of the CPA types she ran into were dead. That sort of thinking led one place—to the big, looming cloud that proclaimed "dateless for twenty-three days now." Definitely not where she wanted to go. As simple as it would be to tread into deeper waters with a sweet guy like Henson, she saw the risks a mile away.

He was one of those guys who wanted something *permanent*. The only things in her life that were permanent were her friends and her work. And that was fine by her.

"I didn't think this guy had any family," Henson tacked on just to add credibility to his question and to prompt an answer, which he would already know. It was his job to know. Charlie Crane's death might just be a suicide, but in the state of Florida all unattended deaths had to be investigated, especially those involving trauma.

"The landlord." Her gaze went back to rest on Charlie's slumped form. He had to be sixty at least. It amazed her that he didn't have any family at all. No parents, no kids, no siblings. No one. Not even any real friends as far as the landlord knew. A stir of something Alex refused to identify made her stomach feel a little tight and queasy.

Henson cocked his head and studied the stiff, then tossed her a sympathetic look. "Well, I'm glad it's you and not me. As soon as the M.E.'s finished, I'm out of here." He visibly shuddered.

She considered the spray of blood and brain matter on the paneled wall behind the body. Could have been worse. She'd certainly seen stuff more ghastly than this. "Nothing I haven't done before."

"A guy never knows what a girl's going to like." Henson flashed her another of those big ol' grins he considered charming, but she hadn't missed the hint of bitterness in his voice.

"You could always stay and watch, you might learn something more about what this girl likes," she challenged. As she suspected, the big, brave cop didn't have anything to say to that, for more reasons than the work that lay ahead of her.

She realized it sounded strange, but the fallout

from the manner of death didn't really bother her. The bodies, well that was a different matter. Somehow seeing the person, or what was left of the person, made her knees go a little weak. The way they did now. She fought hard not to let Henson see her inner reaction to the corpse that hadn't been taken away yet. She had a reputation to maintain after all. Not to mention she went through this routine every time she showed up at a scene. Men just couldn't believe that women could handle seeing something this gruesome even though women were the ones who more often than not changed dirty diapers. Go figure.

Not surprisingly, a lot of people asked how she got into the business of dealing with dead things. She usually made a joke of it. Someone had to do it, right? Truth was, her first experience cleaning up after the recently deceased had come at the ripe old age of fifteen. She hadn't had a lot of choice in the matter. It was either jump in and help her mother or stand back and watch her do it alone. Alex hadn't been able to do that…her mother had needed her, but she would have cut out her tongue before she would have asked her daughter for help. That moment had fore-shadowed more than Alex's future occupation; she'd been taking care of her mother in one way or another ever since.

As with Alex's current assignment, her father hadn't chosen the tidiest way to end his pathetic existence. A slightly off-center shot to the chest where the lungs could have sucked in most of the blood would have been preferable and considerably simpler. But like everything else in her life, his suicide hadn't been simple. A single shot to the head using a 30.06 rifle created an explosion that made a mess of the crappy room in the dilapidated house they'd called home. He'd been an alcoholic who couldn't see past the hole he'd dug himself into, so he'd taken the easy way out.

Considering her line of work, Alex supposed you could say the event had made an impact on her. So, after dropping out of college—she hadn't fit in and money always seemed to be an issue—and drifting from one dead-end job to the other, she started her own business, Never Happened. Another cop she'd dated once had given her the idea and all the reason in the world she would ever need *not* to date cops. Still, she'd ended up dating Henson. Their relationship hadn't lasted the month and it was over more than three months ago. Truth was, it never should have started. When it came to men, apparently she had a faulty memory.

Giving credit where credit was due, that first cop had given her something to think about. What happened when a person committed suicide or died of natural causes or, God forbid, was murdered and wasn't found in a timely manner? Who cleaned up the mess? In the past it was usually a family member, but today, with elderly folks who have no family left or with those too busy to maintain family ties, who cleaned up the mess?

More often than not, there were diseases to worry about, and in the cases of advanced decomposition, normal body fluids could become toxic, making it dangerous for a regular Joe to do the cleanup.

All she'd had to do was get licensed in the cleanup and disposal of hazardous materials, learn to use the right cleaners and equipment and she was good to go. Her phone hadn't stopped ringing since. For the first time in her life she'd become totally self-sufficient and was her own boss. She wouldn't get rich but she did well enough to keep her bills paid and a skeleton crew of local misfits in work, including one of her closest high school friends—who assuredly would not be pleased at being lumped in with the rest of the group.

And, Alex still helped out her mother, who was fifty-five now. She was a recovering alcoholic as of last year and Alex spent far too much of her time keeping her that way. But she had to give her mother credit for helping out with the business in a way that Alex wasn't sure she would be particularly good at. Though she refused to go near a dead body, Margie Jackson was a damned good public relations rep. She single-handedly took care of all advertising and special offers, like fifty percent off a second service.

Believe it or not, there were people who liked getting unsightly spots removed from carpet and the like in rooms other than the cleanup scene when Alex or one of her associates showed up to handle the remains of a dead relative or tenant.

Never Happened was a broad-spectrum cleanup service. They cleaned up most anything. Calls generally involved someone's passing, whether by natural causes or those not so natural. There was the occasional meth lab deserted by some scumbag who had or hadn't gotten caught. Once in a while Alex got a request from folks who had experienced some sort of animal invasion, like a gator gaining access through an open patio door and getting swallowed by the family's pet Burmese python. Big snake. Big mess.

Two carcasses to remove. Then there were part-time residents who returned to their vacation home to find that rats had taken over during the off-season. You'd be surprised at the number of people who would rather die than sweep up a little rat poop.

She supposed that was why they called Miami the international playground of the rich and famous. Folks had money for most anything they desired, which was real nice for Alex and her business.

Never Happened provided a necessary service to the community.

When the victim's cause of death fell outside "natural causes" or was unattended, like now, Alex had no choice but to wait until the police had done their job to get started on hers. The delay made the scene a little less pleasant, but there were masks for that.

Outside, in her shamelessly overpriced Toyota 4Runner, she carried the accessories of the trade. Hazmat—hazardous materials—outfits and bags for carrying away the refuse. The outfits weren't attractive by any stretch of the imagination, think beekeeper, but like the bags they worked and that was what mattered. Assorted neutralizers, protein-stain cleaners, various tools and rags, as well as enzyme cleaners that killed blood-borne bacteria and pathogens equipped her for the job. Not exactly the Lysol and bleach one used at home, but the objective was the same.

A full forty-five minutes and a latte later—Henson insisted on sending one of his minions to the Starbucks on the corner since Alex was forced to wait—the M.E. showed up and took charge of the body, which was wholly his jurisdiction.

She and Henson stayed out of the way, during which time she listened to how he'd installed French doors in his living room over the weekend and how he'd love it if she stopped by to see what a great job he'd done. He still wanted to be friends. She wanted that, as well, but feared it would never be enough for him in the long run and that moment would be painful so she steered clear of getting too close again.

With a promise to have a look very soon, Alex watched the cops and the M.E. head out. Since the M.E. had pronounced the cause of death as probably suicide and the police hadn't found any indication of foul play she could do what she'd come to do: Make the small paneled den look as if a suicide had never happened on the premises.

She had no preset amount of time to spend on the job; each one was different. First she donned the requisite suit, including shoe covers, safety glasses and gloves, then she surveyed the scene. Mentally noted the areas where matter had sprayed outside the anticipated range. Checked under furniture and behind curtains and blinds. No one wanted to enter a room and discover human remains clinging to the underside of a blind slat. Definitely not a good thing.

"Aha." Alex grunted with the effort it took to fish what she was relatively certain was an eyeball out from under a chair. When the object rolled, covered in dust bunnies, into the open, she knew she'd been right. In cases such as this, it wasn't unusual for parts to be overlooked. Unless there was reason to suspect foul play, it wasn't necessary to round up every speck of DNA.

Alex shook her head and reached for her hazmat bag. Just before she chucked the eyeball, something other than dust on the surface caught her attention.

She tried to lift it loose but her gloves wouldn't allow for the fine motor effort. Carrying the eyeball loosely in the palm of her hand she went in search of tweezers.

After a few frustrating failures she finally lifted what looked like a contact lens off the delicate surface. She dropped the eyeball in the hazmat bag but kept the lens to examine it further. This was no ordinary vision enhancer. This sucker was way thicker than the usual lens. Then again, the victim had been well past his prime. But even someone half-blind wouldn't have needed a lens this thick and, now that she thought about it, large. The damned thing was as big as a nickel.

And there was something metallic looking around the edges. Very strange, kind of sci-fi-like.

She was pretty sure Henson would think she was nuts, but she wasn't taking any chances. She'd had the same briefing everyone in her line of work received. Anything suspicious should be reported. No exceptions. No hesitation.

Alex bagged the lens and, after removing her right glove, used her cell to call Henson. He answered on the second ring.

"Hey, Henson, this is Alex." She stared at the object in the bag and hesitated, but only for a second. "Look, I found an eyeball from the vic."

He chuckled. "The guy blew his brains out. The M.E. shouldn't have any trouble confirming cause of death without an eyeball. Just toss it."

Alex rolled her eyes. She'd known he would get in a crack of some sort. Henson was one of those guys who thought he had a stand-up comic's sense of humor. She was too nice to tell him any different. Apparently so was everyone else he knew and worked with. He would make a good husband and father. She'd had that same thought more than once during their brief "thing." But she wasn't into commitment. Maybe that's why she'd backed off so quickly.

Where the hell had that thought come from? She gave herself a mental slap on the forehead. She wasn't afraid of commitment…she just wasn't interested.

"It's not the eyeball that I'm calling about." She frowned, studying the lens more closely. "The guy was wearing some kind of weird contact lens. I've never seen anything like it. Maybe it's nothing, but I think you need to see this for yourself."

After the usual joke about how some ladies would come up with any kind of excuse to enjoy his company, he promised to swing back by the scene pronto.

Alex put her phone away, stashed the lens in a safe place, and did what she'd come there to do.

She was nearly finished wiping away the ugly event by the time Henson showed up.

"Had another call," he said by way of apology for his tardiness.

She lifted her shoulders. "No problem. I'll be here a little longer."

He looked around, made one of those sounds that meant *wow*, and said, "It's hard to believe it comes this clean."

She handed him the Ziploc bag. "Where there's a will there's a way."

His typical comeback wasn't forthcoming; he was too busy visually examining the lens or whatever the hell it was.

"Weird, huh?" Alex couldn't help feeling a little vindicated by his apparent interest.

Too preoccupied to respond, he squinted to make out more details. Finally he said, "It looks almost like some kind of computer chip." His gaze met hers. "You say this was on the guy's eye?"

She nodded. "Stuck on the surface, over the iris, just like a contact lens." She'd forgotten that Henson was big into the whole electronics-techno world.

"I'll have it checked out. I've got a buddy over in Morningside who's deep into computer technology. Stays on the very edge of what's new and hot. Maybe he can at least identify what it is. He's done this kind of thing for me before. He loves this stuff." Henson arrowed a knowing look at Alex. "The kid should be working at the state crime lab. He's that good and he's fast."

She'd done her good deed for the day and wanted to get on with her work and get out of there. "Let me know what you find out."

Clearly still in a world of his own, Henson nodded as he turned away. "Will do."

He left without another last-ditch attempt to entice her to go out with him, without even a *see ya around*. That was just like a man. No matter that for months he'd endeavored to woo her to go on another date, he could still be distracted by a new toy.

After a few more minutes of elbow grease and a final look around, Alex decided it was as good as it was going to get. The only thing she hadn't been able to rectify was the bullet hole in the paneling. It might not have been so noticeable if the forensics tech hadn't gouged the bullet out of the two-by-four it had lodged itself into. Drywall she could repair; paneling, that was a whole other problem. Maybe the landlord could hang a picture on the wall to cover the damage or fill it and just paint the whole room.

Now for her least favorite part of the job; collecting payment. This business was cash-and-carry, no thirty days to pay, strictly payment due at time of services. She did accept Visa and MasterCard, though, and, if she knew the individual well enough, personal checks. As much as she disliked this part, it was essential to get payment as quickly as possible since it was all too easy for money to end up spent on the living.

She dropped the hazmat bags containing the refuse, all the cleaning rags associated with the job, as well as the suit, gloves and shoe covers she'd worn, at the disposal center then headed to the landlord's property office. With her payment collected she was done for the day.

Maybe she'd stop by the office on the way home and maybe she wouldn't. Right now a shower and then a long hot bath sounded far too inviting to waste time sparring with her crew. It was past closing time anyway. Most would be out of there already.

Tomorrow was another day, and in a teeming city like Miami, as well as all its suburbs, where drug deals went wrong and gangs got even, there was always plenty of job security for a woman in her line of work.

Cleaning up after the dead wasn't exactly a market one had to fear would dry up.

CHAPTER 2

Twelve miles of calm waters, clean sands and swaying palm trees. Alex breathed deeply of the late-summer evening air as she cruised along Ocean Boulevard, allowing that saltwater essence to clean the stench of death from her lungs. God, she loved everything about Miami Beach. Maybe she didn't live in one of the upscale art deco homes in this world-renowned neighborhood, but she didn't care. This was home…stunning, intoxicating…and forever youthful.

Age was irrelevant here. No one cared how old you were because everyone dressed and behaved young at heart. Whether they were soaking up the rays or haunting the designer shops, locals and tourists alike sauntered to the beat of a different tune—one filled with Latin heat and the primal lust of the tropical landscape.

She leaned against the headrest and let the

pleasant breeze caress her face. The perfect climate
and the lush scenery might draw the world to Miami
but it was the eclectic blend of people that made this
city so unique. Cubans, Colombians, Peruvians and
Venezuelans made up fifty percent of the population. Not surprising that Spanish was the primary
language. The news from Havana or Caracas was
more often than not the talk on the street.

Speaking of people, as traffic slowed near 10th
Street, Alex braked and watched couples glide into
the Casa Casuarina, a hotel that was once home to
the revered designer Gianni Versace. Not even the
fabulous architecture could detract from the gorgeous
patrons flowing into the ritzy joint. Men with wash-
board stomachs and bulging pecs were outfitted in
the still famous *Miami Vice* Sonny Crockett look
with their loose-fitting linen slacks and silk shirts.
Soft pastels were sharply contrasted by richly tanned
skin. Alex sighed as she studied the appetizing smor-
gasbord of pleasing male specimens. Just part of the
everyday landscape and another aspect of her love
affair with this city. She wasn't intimidated in the
least by the equally attractive ladies with their short,
tight dresses and stiletto heels.

Beneath her faded jeans and Margaritaville tee,

Alex maintained the kind of figure women half her age envied. She knew it, reveled in it. She'd learned a long time ago that humility was vastly overrated. If you had it, you saw it for what it was and used the hell out of it. Life was too short to do otherwise.

Admittedly it took work to stay in this kind of physical condition, she mused as her right foot instinctively pressed against the accelerator, propelling her SUV forward with the traffic. After all she wasn't twenty anymore.

A sly grin slid across her face. But she wasn't dead, either. Nor was she wearing her age on her sleeve, so to speak. She liked keeping the world guessing. Only two people in her life knew her exact age; her oldest and dearest friend, who had been sworn to secrecy under fear of death; and her mother, who wouldn't dare tell her daughter's age for fear of giving away her own.

With a final, longing look at one particular man on the busy sidewalk, Alex made the necessary turn and headed toward a less glamorous residential district. The working-class side of town. Art deco remained the prevailing theme in architecture, even in her lower rent neighborhood but with a more Bohemian atmosphere. Her small cottage wasn't on the water, but there was a boardwalk nearby that went all the way to the water's edge. Anywhere around here was close to the ocean—that living, breathing entity upon which this city thrived.

She pulled into the short driveway and slid out of the 4Runner. No, it wasn't much, she thought with a frank yet appreciative survey of the property, but it was home and it was hers. Her grandmother had left it to her. Alex grabbed her bag, elbowed the door closed and clicked the remote lock.

Sometimes she felt guilty that she'd inherited the cottage instead of her mother. But her grandmother—her mother's own mother—had known that Margie Jackson would piss the property away if given the chance.

As if fate had chosen that memory to warn that trouble was headed her way, Alex's cell erupted with the chorus from "It's Getting Hot in Here" by Nelly.

She checked the caller ID. "Damn." The office. Had to be Shannon, her office manager and lifelong best friend. This couldn't be good. It was almost six. "Hey, Shannon, what's up?" Alex shoved the key into the lock of her front door. If the news was really bad she wanted to be within arm's reach of a cold one.

"We may have a potential problem, Alexis."

Definitely bad. Shannon only called her Alexis when she wanted her full attention.

Putting off the inevitable, Alex walked straight through the cluttered and cozy living room to the equally disorganized and cramped kitchen before she responded, "Oh yeah?" She snagged a Michelob from the fridge and twisted off the top. Not wanting Shannon's announcement to get too far ahead of the alcohol, Alex chugged a long swallow. The brew made her shiver as much from the promise of a relaxing buzz it offered as the cold temperature.

With her hip, she closed the fridge door, leaned against it and pressed the chilly bottle to the damp skin at her throat. Okay, so maybe there was one thing about Miami she could live without: humidity. You couldn't exist in this city without sweating. Day, night, working out or just sitting still.

"He asked her out for a third date."

All thoughts of sweat and the most pleasurable ways to manufacture a healthy glaze on one's skin vanished as her friend's words penetrated fully.

"When? Today?"

"He called just before she left the office." Shannon

sighed. "You should have heard her, she giggled like a schoolgirl. She was all giddy…you know how she gets. I see trouble on the horizon, Alex. Big trouble."

Damn. Alex shook her head. "You couldn't stop her?"

"Right," Shannon retorted. "Your mother has been on the wagon for more than a year. I value my life more than that. I have kids you know."

"Your kids are grown, Shannon."

Ignoring Alex's reply, her friend covertly added, "I know where they were going."

Alex pushed away from the fridge and headed for the bedroom. Might as well get this over with. She could either head off this train wreck or pick up the pieces afterward. "Where?"

It wouldn't be the first time she'd had to rescue her mother. Probably wouldn't be the last. Life could be complicated when you were the only child of a re-covering alcoholic.

"Ruby's."

"Thanks, Shannon."

"What're you going to do?"

Alex took another pull from her beer and set it on the dresser as she crossed her room. "What I usually do." She closed her phone without saying more.

Further explanation wasn't necessary; Shannon understood what she meant.

Alex stared at her reflection a moment and wondered what her life would have been like if things had been different. Had watching her parents fight nonstop until the night her father killed himself, kept her single and glad to be that way? Or had her mother's string of failed relationships turned Alex cynical when it came to anything long-term?

If life had taken a different turn for her, would Alex have kids off in college now like Shannon? A husband who spent his Saturdays watching sports? Sex every third Sunday of the month?

Alex shuddered at the concept.

God must have known she wasn't cut out for that kind of life. Just to make sure she veered far away from unnecessary commitments; life tossed her the occasional reminder, such as this one. Some people simply shouldn't be spouses, much less parents. Unfortunately her mother was one of those people.

Alex ripped off her T-shirt and shimmied out of her jeans. Shower or no, she couldn't go to Ruby's looking like one of the guys.

* * *

It never ceased to amaze Alex just how good a hardworking woman could look if she put her mind to it. Even if she'd spent the better part of the day scraping human remains off a wall.

Good genes were the one reliable thing her mother had given her.

After parking on the Washington Avenue side of the establishment, Alex walked into Ruby's Lounge with all the confidence of a supermodel. Her dress was black and short with heels high enough to make a lesser woman acrophobic, but not Alex. She'd fashioned her long blond hair into a sexy French twist. Her lips twitched. She loved anything French, including the men. Thank God for European tourists.

She surveyed the tables of the lounge, which was a throwback to a bygone era. Some tables were wrapped with comfy sofas for more intimate dining, while others stood tall and were surrounded by stools. Every seat was taken. Latin salsa throbbed from the sound system as waiters and waitresses wove through the maze of bodies and tables.

"Do you have a reservation?"

Alex smiled for the host, garnering herself an approving smile in return. "I'm afraid I can't stay," she said wistfully. "I'm only here to relay a message to a friend."

"Your friend's name?"

She held up a hand. "It's all right. I see her."

It wasn't as if it was difficult. Her mother's boisterous laugh stood out in a crowd like the proverbial sore thumb. Same blond hair as her daughter's, only shorter. Alex's gaze narrowed as she took in the pink suit. Apparently her mother had raided her closet. They would be talking about that.

Alex strode to the table. The new boyfriend looked up as she paused next to her mother's chair.

"Alex! How nice to see you."

The way his gaze slid down her body as he spoke told her he meant the statement literally.

"Robert." She gave him a plastic smile before turning her attention to her mother. "Marg, may I have a word with you in private."

Margie Jackson, who had refused to allow her daughter to call her mother once she became a widow, looked suspicious of her offspring's abrupt appearance. "Alex, what a surprise."

Alex's determined stare apparently provided a recognizable caveat that she wasn't leaving until they talked, here or in private.

Marg stood. "Excuse me, Robert."

Robert nodded, the glint in his eyes giving away his infinite hope that both women would return post-haste, perhaps naked and pleading with him to take them straight to his place.

Like that was going to happen in this lifetime.

Alex led the way to the ladies' room. She checked the stalls to make sure they were alone, then rounded on her mother. "What the hell are you doing?"

Marg glared at her daughter. "Stop right there. I'm not drinking, Alex. I'm done with that life. I like Robert and I want to get to know him better. You cannot expect me to live my new, *clean* life alone. I have needs."

Alex wished she could believe that. "This is your third date with dear old Robert," she reminded. "You know what that means."

Her mother looked away, even had the gall to blush. "Alex, my social life is none of your business."

If only that were the way of things, but it wasn't. Her hands on her hips, Alex moved in closer. "Mother, I've known you—"

"Don't call me that," Marg chastised.

"—my entire life." Alex forged ahead. "You always have sex on the third date." She held up her hands to stop Marg from protesting. "For whatever reason, after copulating the night away, the relationship ends and you turn to the bottle for solace. In twenty-five years I've never seen you deviate from that pattern. Three dates, sex—bam—you're out!"

Marg crossed her arms firmly over her Pamela-Anderson-size bosom—a Christmas present to herself last year. "Alexis Jackson, you have no right to dictate my sex life to me. I haven't had sex in over a year! For God's sake, I'm lonely!"

The door opened and a woman came inside. She glanced at the two and hurried into a stall.

"Be that as it may," Alex replied, "I know how this will end. You and physical relationships don't mix. There are alternatives," she added in a whisper.

"It's not the same," her mother snapped.

Okay, this was bizarre, Alex knew. She was in a public restroom—in a lounge of all places—having the sex talk with her mother, a woman far beyond the age of consent. And she was right. The alternatives just weren't the same. Some people had problems with gambling, others with weight or drugs. Her mother simply couldn't have a physical relationship with a man without turning to alcohol. The combination was always, always disastrous. And Alex invariably had to clean up afterward.

"I'm going back out there," Marg said, her expression fierce, maybe even a little desperate, "and I don't want to hear anything else about this. I'm way past three times seven, Alex. I don't need you telling me what to do. And I certainly don't need your permission."

Unable to allow her mother to have the last word, Alex said the one thing she knew would have the most impact, "Don't say I didn't warn you."

Alex walked out, didn't look back, didn't even slow until she'd hit the unlock button for her 4Runner on the opposite side of the block.

Some women just never learned. When you recognized a weakness, you avoided it, learned from your previous mistakes.

Alex slid behind the wheel and exhaled a heavy breath. That was the primary difference between her and her mother, besides the store-bought triple-D cups. No man would ever make Alex that vulnerable.

Never.

She loved men, enjoyed dating every chance she got. But she never allowed a relationship to develop beyond the physical. Most men didn't have a problem with that. Only once in a really long time had she been forced to let a guy down and he still hadn't given up completely. Henson, damn him. He'd almost weakened her defenses. Thank God she'd come to her senses in time. Commitment was *not* her gig.

She twisted the key in the ignition and pulled out onto the street. Time for that long, steamy bath she'd had to put off to come here and do her daughterly duty.

Maybe one of these days her mother would learn that some things just weren't meant to be.

Thirty minutes later, hot, frothy water up to her neck, a cold bottle of Michelob in her hand, Alex had finally relaxed fully. She refused to think about the trouble her mother would likely get into before this night was over.

She refused to think at all. It wasn't her problem…yet.

Candles were lit, the air was thick with steam. This moment made the day's dirty work worth the effort. A bubble bath was her favorite way to soothe away the day's stress. Well, there were other ways, but at least this one never failed her.

There she went again thinking about sex. No date in three weeks. It was oddly unsettling. Was she subconsciously going for a record? Nah. Just coincidence. It wasn't as if sex was like vitamins, she didn't have to have it every day.

She closed her eyes and let the water melt the tension. Her place didn't have a lot to offer in the way of amenities, not even a dishwasher, but it did have this huge tub in the master bath. And there was no mortgage. Two very important assets in a single woman's life.

The wood floors guaranteed she'd never have to worry about replacing carpet. The tile roof and stucco exterior ensured that, outside of being hit by a hurricane, nothing more than a paint job would ever be required. The lack of fancy appliances promised nothing expensive would break down. The furniture was the same overstuffed, worn pieces her grandmother had owned forever. And the tiny apartment over the garage provided a place to keep her mother off the streets.

Alex was pretty sure her grandmother had planned it that way, and her mother didn't really seem to mind. She evidently understood on some level that she couldn't be trusted as a home owner. Besides, the whole setup gave her total freedom from responsibility.

The creak of a floorboard somewhere beyond the

half-open bathroom door jolted Alex from her mental ramblings. She sat up straight and listened.

Another squeak had her climbing quietly out of the water and reaching for her robe. She slipped into her bedroom and grabbed the can of pepper spray from the bedside table and eased closer to the door.

Since she didn't carry a gun, the pepper spray was her weapon of choice. This was Miami after all. It hadn't been that long ago that it was the murder capital of the nation. She had no intention of becoming a victim and going down without a fight.

When she heard no other sounds, Alex moved through the door and into the short hall that separated her bedroom from the living room-kitchen area. The house was silent. She liked it that way when she wanted to relax, enjoyed listening to the night sounds. Even hearing the neighbors arguing at the house next door was somehow comforting and innately familiar.

Being careful not to make any noise, she moved through each room to ensure there wasn't an intruder. Doors, front and back, were still locked. Windows were open, the night breeze shifting the curtains but nothing looked out of the ordinary. Slowly she let down her guard. With the windows up the sound could have carried from next door; the houses on either side of her had wooden porches.

Alex returned to her bedroom and opened her lingerie drawer. When she would have selected a clean pair of underwear, she hesitated. Something wasn't right. Her pulse skipped as she checked drawer after drawer. Everything was there but different somehow...as if someone had riffled through her things.

The pink suit flashed in her mind and realization made a delayed appearance.

She was going to kill her mother.

Not only had she borrowed the pink skirt and jacket, but clearly she'd made herself at home with Alex's undergarments.

She hoped Robert enjoyed them.

A car door slammed outside. Alex's head came up and she listened.

Her mother's voice. Robert's.

Alex tiptoed over to the window and peeked past the edge of the curtain. The streetlamp spotlighted Robert's efforts to pull Marg into his arms, but she resisted. Alex's jaw dropped. Since when was playing hard to get part of her mother's third-date routine?

She heard Marg say good-night, then watched in astonishment as she strode up the walk and across the yard to the exterior stairs that led up to her apartment without a single hesitation or backward glance.

Alone.

Unbelievable.

Robert stared after her a few moments before getting into his sleek sports car and driving off.

"Hot damn!"

Maybe her mother had finally gotten her act together.

Alex owed her an apology.

She was woman enough to admit when she was wrong.

With that in mind, she strode out her front door and straight up the stairs to her mother's door. Just before she knocked, the music beyond stopped her.

Ten seconds passed before she recognized the music from the workout video *Sweating to the Oldies*.

Alex smiled.

Dear old Richard Simmons.

Grinning, she did an about-face and went back to her own home. Apparently her mother had opted for one of the alternatives Alex had mentioned. An extensive physical workout could go a long way in alleviating certain types of stress.

"Good girl," she muttered as she closed and locked her own front door behind her.

Maybe you could teach an old dog new tricks.

The jangle of her landline disturbed the pleasant silence and annoyance flared. It was late, she was ready for bed. Who the hell would call her at this time of night? The answer was not the one she wanted. Work most likely.

She didn't want to know about any more trouble.

"Alex Jackson." She'd stopped answering with hello years ago. It seemed all her regular customers, various landlords, cops and whatnot, assumed her home number was a business number, too.

"Hey, Alex, it's Rich."

Henson. What did he want? Guilt pinged her. She didn't actually mind hearing from him, but she'd learned from experience that maintaining frequent contact proved nothing more than a segue to *let's try again*. She pulled the lapels of her robe together, suddenly self-conscious that she was naked under this robe. Was that dumb or what? After three months you would think she'd have her head straight about this guy. He wanted commitment and she didn't…but he'd made her wonder what if? No other man had ever managed to do that. Everything had been fine until today.

"What's up?" She was careful to keep her tone light, but clearly disinterested in anything other than straightforward conversation. She mentally weighed the pros and cons of having another beer. Three was usually her limit, but this night had the definite makings of a six-packer.

"I just wanted to call and thank you for alerting me to that piece of evidence you found this afternoon."

She hesitated at the fridge and her forehead pinched with a frown. Was this call really about business? "The contact lens?" Okay, so maybe they could have a chat without the inevitable invitation to pick up where they left off.

"Apparently it's some sort of computer chip. I'm on my way over to Morningside to pick it up from that whiz kid I told you about. He's done some quick unofficial analysis for me before. I wanted to be sure this was something worth using taxpayers' dollars to analyze. I'll be taking it straight to the state lab tomorrow, but you know how slow they are to respond. This kind of heads-up will get the ball rolling. Outstanding call, Alex."

"That's great." She didn't know why it mattered or what exactly his obvious excitement meant, but she was glad Henson was happy about it. The moment gave her hope that maybe they could actually be just friends.

"Anyway," he went on, his enthusiasm palpable, "I thought maybe you'd let me take you to dinner on Friday night to repay the good deed."

Oh, man. There it was. Her hopes deflated. The man would never give up.

"I'd love to, Henson, but unfortunately I already have plans for Friday night." It was true. She'd promised to go to a movie with Shannon; the woman swore if she didn't have ladies' night out once a month she'd go mad. Alex felt reasonably certain she wasn't exaggerating.

"Another time maybe," he said.

She nodded, to convince herself evidently since he couldn't see her. "Another time…maybe." She hated constantly turning him down. He really was a nice guy. She didn't get why he didn't just give up. He deserved someone who wanted the same sort of commitments he did. She was not that girl.

"Well, look. I'm getting another call. 'Night, Alex."

"G'night, Henson."

As she hung up the phone she couldn't have guessed in a million years that it would be the last time she would talk to Detective Rich Henson.

CHAPTER 3

The offices of Never Happened sat way, way, way off Ocean Boulevard. Not a bad location but a bit off the beaten path, nestled between the office of Dr. Sherman Holloway, psychologist extraordinaire, and Patsy's Clip Joint, a pet salon. Things could get a little noisy at times, otherwise the folks on either side of Alex's offices were pretty easy to get along with.

There was, however, the perpetual parking problem. The alley between Never Happened and Patsy's was supposed to be shared space, except her clients weren't always so considerate. Especially the ones with the big, luxury automobiles and the small, prissy dogs.

Alex rolled into what she had claimed as her space next to the brick wall of her building. Since most of her staff arrived before seven, morning parking wasn't usually a problem. Afternoons were a different story, however; things could get hairy.

She pulled down the visor and checked her reflection in the mirror. Eyeliner, lipstick, no smears or smudges. Good to go. Flipping the visor back into place, she grabbed her knockoff gold Fendi shoulder bag, her caramel-mocha latte and climbed out of her SUV.

As she turned the corner toward her shop front, a long low whistle trilled behind her.

"My, my, Alex," Patsy called from the open entrance of her shop, "don't you look sharp today." Her wolf call had prompted a cacophony of yelps from her restless four-legged guests.

Alex smiled. "Thanks." The low-slung jeans she wore were her favorite. She'd paired them with thonged sandals and a ribbed pullover that didn't quite reach the extrawide belt buckled around her waist. "You've lost more weight," Alex commented after giving her business neighbor an approving once-over.

"Forty pounds so far," Patsy confirmed before a lengthy drag on her Kool 100 Ultra Light. "Twenty-five more to go. I'm itching for that new wardrobe my husband promised me. Give me a couple more months and we'll set a shopping date. I'd love a day away from this." She jerked her head toward the racket inside.

Alex gave her the thumbs-up before heading into her office. According to Patsy she'd been overweight her whole life; with forty breathing down her neck now she'd decided enough was enough. She didn't want to plunge into middle age as a fat woman with climbing cholesterol and soaring triglycerides. Alex admired her determination. Change was good…for some people. Personally, she liked her life exactly as it was.

Most of the time.

"'Morning, Alex."

Though her lifelong friend and office manager, Shannon, had tried her level best not to glance at the clock, she did. She couldn't help herself. Alex had known Shannon Bainbridge since kindergarten when she was mild-mannered Shannon Owens. The woman had always been as sweet and kind as any angel, but she was an obsessive-compulsive, Type-A personality, perfectionist to the max.

"It's seven-oh-two but I'm here," Alex said in acknowledgement of her silent chastisement. "Good morning to you, too."

"Guten morgen, Alexis."

Alex shifted her attention to the man lounging on the sofa and perusing today's *Miami Herald*. "Same to you, Professor." He liked showing off his command of various languages. So far she'd recognized six. She'd hired the Professor, aka Barton Winstead III, four years ago when he'd "defected," as he called it, to Florida from his homeland of Boston. He'd left his career in anthropology behind, as well. To this day Alex had no idea at which university he'd taught or the reason for his decision to leave. He didn't talk about it, she didn't ask. She liked him. He had that distinguished look about him. Even his thinning gray hair added an air of dignity. But it was the extreme intelligence that radiated from those caring hazel eyes that she liked most.

"Marg hasn't come in yet, and Madonna is waiting in your office." Shannon glanced up from the computer monitor and peered knowingly at Alex over her reading glasses. *"She's not happy."*

"She's never happy," the Professor noted aloud, his regard remaining fixed on today's headlines as if he hadn't made the aside.

"Perfect." Alex braced for battle and headed for her office. If she hadn't been running behind herself this morning she might have noticed that Marg hadn't left yet, either. Alex just loved starting her morning off with worries about Marg.

Never Happened was made up of only four rooms. Reception in front, which wasn't that large, about sixteen by twenty, a narrow hall that led to Alex's office, really small, an even dinkier lounge directly across the hall from her, which her mother used as a sort of office, and a huge storeroom which occupied the rest of the building and included an employee's restroom and a side exit to the alley. The latter had been the key selling point for Alex. All her supplies were housed in that storeroom. The handy side exit leading to the alley allowed for easy loading and unloading of the necessary materials for any given assignment.

Unlike the neighbor's less than considerate pet owners, most knew better than to park in front of an entrance or an exit. Especially since the city's Dumpster sat right outside the door. Two days per week the south end of the alley remained clear all day; there wasn't a Miami driver around who would dare challenge a garbage truck on pickup day.

The interior of Alex's portion of the building was nothing to brag about. No fancy carpet or paint job. Just practical commercial tile on the floor and plain white walls with little or no decorating. The business license and various other permits hung on the wall above the front counter that separated Shannon's desk from the sofa and two chairs that served as lobby seating. Shannon had donated the sofa and coordinating chairs the last time she'd redecorated her den. Alex had purchased the rest of the mismatched furnishings at garage sales and business closeouts.

She gulped another drink of her latte for courage and reached for the knob of her closed door. Might as well get this over with. Inside her ten-by-twelve space sat her only other employee, with the exception of her missing mother. Leslie Brown, perched rigidly in the only chair besides the one behind Alex's desk, heaved an impatient breath as if the boss's arrival was long overdue.

Brown wore a double-breasted black suit reminiscent of the one Madonna had donned in her *Vogue* music video. The platinum wig and heavy makeup, including blood-red lips and a black mole, completed the sultry image.

"Good morning, Brown."

He cut Alex a withering look.

"Excuse me. *Madonna*," Alex amended as she scooted around the corner of her desk and dropped her bag onto the only vacant spot on the floor near her chair. After grabbing a quick sip of her latte, she pushed aside a stack of papers and set the cup in the cleared spot. To say her office was cluttered would be a monumental understatement. Files, including incoming shipment invoices and outgoing payment receipts, were stacked on the corners of her desk, but it was the test products, many still in their boxes, sitting here and there around the room that made maneuvering the most difficult. Shannon hated it. Threatened Alex all the time about the chaos. But Alex knew where everything was. She rarely lost anything.

"So." Giving Brown her undivided attention, Alex propped her elbows on her desk and laced her fingers. "What seems to be the problem this morning?"

Brown lifted his chin defiantly. "I need Friday off and Shannon refuses to okay my request." The thick Latino intonation made his every word more resounding.

That was odd. Unless something came up, giving him a day off with advance notice wasn't generally a problem. Unless Shannon knew something Alex didn't, she didn't see the problem. "I'll see what I can do," she promised. Didn't sound like a big deal. She relaxed. This had certainly proven far easier than she'd expected. Generally if Brown had a problem, it was a little more daunting.

Unfortunately, judging by the look on Brown's face and the fact that he made no move to leave her office, Alex had counted her chickens before they hatched.

He leaned forward and warned, "It's because of the convention. She doesn't want me to participate. She can't do that." He tapped his chest in the vicinity of what Alex could only imagine was a heavily padded bra providing the hill and valley effect of breasts. "I know my rights," he warned.

Alex snapped her gaze back up to his irate expression; a bad feeling churned in her gut. "What convention?"

"The Ms. Miami convention. I've been signed up for weeks. Don't you remember? You sponsored me. Friday is the first day. Registration and screening. I have to be there."

Alex struggled to swallow back her first reaction. She vaguely remembered sponsoring him for some sort of convention, she just didn't remember it was this particular convention. "Not—" she cleared her throat "—a problem. I'll take care of it."

"Fine." Brown stood. Smoothed a hand over his elegant and decidedly feminine jacket. "I hope you'll come to cheer me on."

Alex managed a nod.

Brown hesitated at the door. "I'll send Shannon in to see you so you can tell her right away."

Alex felt her head move up and down again, the smile frozen on her lips.

Twisting his narrow hips with all he had, Brown flounced out of her office.

Alex took a breath, told herself she was cool with this. It was a free country after all. No reason Brown shouldn't go after his heart's desires. It wasn't as if she was ashamed of him or had a problem with his alternative lifestyle.

Okay, that was a lie. She didn't have a problem with it as long as he didn't bring it to work in a way that would hamper business. There simply was no way to have him, without having his eccentricity— it was a package deal. But using his stint in the Ms. Miami pageant as a possible means of advertisement was definitely previously unexplored territory.

Shannon walked in, closed the door behind her. "He told you."

Before Alex could stop the words, she demanded in something that should have been a whisper but came out more like a muffled shout, "Don't you have to be a woman to enter that thing?"

Shannon shrugged her shoulders dramatically. "How the hell do I know? Should I call and ask?"

Alex shook her head adamantly. "We don't want to draw any attention to him or us. Let's just stay calm and pray someone notices at the registration and screening."

Shannon's head bobbed. "How could he win or even get in? I mean—" she lowered her voice to the whisper Alex had been aiming for "—I'll admit that he makes a somewhat attractive woman, but this is a beauty pageant, right? With rules and judges?"

Alex did the bobbing this time. She told herself it wouldn't matter that Brown had killer legs or that his unusually high cheekbones were to die for. "Of course you're right. We have nothing to worry about. No way he'll win. He'll probably be disqualified before the pageant even officially begins."

"Probably."

For about two minutes after Shannon left Alex's office, she pondered the question of why Brown seemed to be confused about his sexuality. Some days he appeared completely happy with his masculinity, others he wanted nothing to do with it, showed up for work as some Hollywood diva. Maybe the good doctor next door could shed some light on the subject. Alex was certain he'd noticed Brown's unusual fashion sense on his feminine days.

Putting her curiosities aside, she turned her attention to the day's schedule. An elderly couple, dead two weeks, had been found in their Coral Gables home. Cause of death was listed as natural by their attending physician so the police wouldn't be holding up the scene. Apparently both had suffered from serious heart conditions. There was no way to be sure who died first, but the death of one of them, evidently, was brought on by the other's fatal attack. With no family in the state to look in on them and the neighbors under the assumption the couple had gone on vacation, no one had realized there was a problem until the stench reared its ugly head.

Brown and the Professor would head out around eight to take care of that one. The family, who'd arrived in town just yesterday, had requested additional services to include cleaning the carpet throughout the home and washing down all walls and ceilings.

Thank God the couple's air-conditioning had kept the house below seventy-five degrees. The mess would be bad enough, but there was nothing as bad as a body that had roasted in Miami's summer heat. The July climate turned a closed-up, non-climate-controlled house into a virtual oven. Not a pleasant situation.

The Professor poked his head through her door. "Have you read the *Herald* this morning?"

Alex tossed the work order aside and picked up her latte to cradle it in her hands. "Haven't had time. Did you find something interesting?" She savored the sweet concoction as she waited expectantly for him to share the news she'd missed.

"I think perhaps you should read this for yourself."

He made the short journey to and around behind her desk. Alex leaned back out of the way while he spread the paper in front of her. He tapped the headline Detective's Death Under Investigation.

"Isn't he a friend of yours?"

Somehow her cup found its way back to her desk as she skimmed the front page article recounting the tragic automobile accident of a longtime criminal investigations detective...

Detective Richard Henson...

"Ohmigod..." Alex looked up at the Professor. "I talked to him last night." *I slept with him three months ago...*

Dread or hurt or something she couldn't quite label welled in her chest. How could this have happened? He'd been fine last night.

The Professor gestured to the paper. "According to the article, the accident likely occurred between eight and ten last night. There aren't that many details given."

Her thoughts whirling, she grappled to recall the approximate time he'd called last night. After Marg had come home. *Sweating to the Oldies*. Alex had considered having another beer.

Eight-fifteen, eight-thirty maybe. Nine at the latest. Jesus.

He could have died only a few minutes after they'd talked. Why hadn't she said…something…like how good it had been to see him that day? Why hadn't she just said yes to dinner?

Henson was dead.

"Thanks, Professor."

Alex didn't notice when he left the room, but he was gone the next time she glanced around her office. She blinked, trying to reconcile herself to what she'd just read.

Henson was really dead.

She forced herself to read the entire article. It

didn't specify the details, but it did mention that the one-car accident was under investigation.

When he'd called he'd said he was going to see the computer whiz kid who'd unofficially analyzed the contact lens.

Had he made it to the guy's house?

Did the police even know where he'd been headed?

Alex sagged in her chair, let the cold, harsh reality wash over her.

Henson was dead.

She was repeating herself but she just couldn't get past it. She'd liked him. Now she'd never get to tell him that if she'd been the type for commitment, he could maybe have been the guy. She should have told him that. But she hadn't. She'd let him believe that he didn't have the "it" she was looking for. That had been a lot easier than explaining what she really felt. She didn't even know what she really felt. She only knew what she didn't want—she didn't want long-term.

No man ever understood that.

Hell, she didn't even understand it, she simply accepted it.

Enough, she ordered. She couldn't sit around here feeling sorry for herself. She had spoken with Henson last night, possibly only minutes before he died. Any information she could offer that might help the investigation was not only her civic duty, it was her obligation as a friend.

Alex finished her latte, grabbed her bag and put thought into action.

The Professor and Brown had this morning's schedule under control. Unless something new came up, she could spare a couple of hours. The final reports she'd been meaning to type and the other paperwork she needed to review could wait.

Her friend was dead.

That wouldn't wait.

The Miami Beach Police station was located at 1100 Washington Avenue in a building that defined the Art Deco style. The Criminal Investigations Unit called the third floor home. The division was laid out in a grid pattern with dozens of metal desks floating amid a sea of beige carpeting. The walls were a matching shade of beige. The only interruption in the beigedom was the stacks of red and blue folders atop the desks. Kind of reminded Alex of her own office.

She waved to a couple of the female detectives she'd worked with on occasion and basically ignored the guys who openly leered. Not that she minded when a man showed his appreciation for her hard work and good genes, but these guys were just being jerks. Most had wives and kids at home.

Yet another reason to stay unattached. You didn't have to worry about a cheating husband if you didn't have one. Didn't have to worry about mismatched socks. Dirty boxers or dishes piled in the sink. Life was just less complicated when one stayed unattached.

She wove through the maze of desks until she reached the one belonging to Detective Jimmy Patton. He and Henson hadn't been partners that long, only since Henson's longtime partner had retired and moved to Maine about six months ago.

When Patton looked up Alex recognized the exhaustion and the pain in his eyes. He'd likely been up all night.

"Jackson," he said, acknowledging her presence but immediately returning his attention to the file in front of him. She was pretty sure his reluctance to maintain eye contact was about keeping his emotions to himself.

"Hey, Patton." She sat down in the chair next to his desk. "I heard about Henson. Man, I can't believe it. Do you know what happened?"

He shook his head, spared her another brief glance. "Techs are...ah...checking out his car for mechanical failures, but it looks like he fell asleep at the wheel. Just ran off the road. He'd been putting in way too many hours lately. I tried to tell him." The sigh that punctuated that final statement as well as his emphatic attempts to refocus his attention on the file gave away just how badly Henson's death had shaken him.

But his words were what hit Alex the hardest. Henson hadn't sounded the least bit sleepy or even tired when she'd spoken to him. In fact, he'd sounded hyped. She couldn't say why, but her intuition was humming like crazy. She'd at first thought that she was merely in denial about Henson's death, but it was more than that.

Stay calm. Take it slow. Hysterics won't get you anywhere. "That's why I came by," she said, unsure whether what she had to say held any relevance but certain she didn't want to keep it to herself in case it proved somehow significant. "Henson called me last night at around eight-thirty, maybe nine."

Patton picked up a small spiral notepad and shuffled through the pages until he'd found what he was looking for. "Yeah, we got that from his cell phone. I know you did a cleanup on an unattended suicide he'd covered. I was going to touch base with you and see if the call he made to you had anything to do with that." His gaze connected with hers then. "Or if maybe the two of you…"

He let the sentence trail off. Alex didn't have to say anything; he read the truth in her eyes. She and Henson hadn't started going out again. Patton looked away as if he'd rather she'd lied to him. Partners talked about their personal lives. She wouldn't have expected any less.

Turning her attention back to the real problem, she asked, "He didn't talk to you last night?" Alex found that possibility unreasonably disturbing considering she'd passed along a piece of possible evidence that Henson had obviously been excited about. Wouldn't he tell his partner that?

Patton scrubbed his hand over his face. "I was at the hospital until I heard about the accident. My wife went into labor a little early."

A new baby. She'd forgotten his wife was expecting. Well that explained his being left out of the loop last night. "Is everything okay?"

He grinned but the effort was a little dim under the circumstances. "Yeah. A girl. Eight pounds one ounce. She's a doll."

Something far too similar to longing pierced a

tender place deep inside Alex. She evicted the sentimental ache and gave herself a swift mental kick for even allowing the senseless emotion to rear its pointless head. She'd made her decisions about husbands and kids long ago. Hearing about other people's kids didn't usually bother her…the emotional roller coaster this morning was about Henson.

She still couldn't believe he was dead. She kept expecting to turn around and hear him tossing some silly joke at her or asking her if she had plans this weekend.

His death had rattled her. This wasn't really about the nonrelationship they'd shared…he was a friend, of course she'd be unsettled by his death. She didn't allow regrets. She preferred her independence. She liked taking care of herself and not having to rely on anyone else for anything. This was just a normal reaction to losing a friend.

Shaking off the disturbing thoughts, she rejoined the conversation and did what she'd come here to do. "I don't know if this makes any difference," she began, unsure exactly how to explain the situation, "but I gave Henson a piece of what may have been evidence from the Crane suicide scene."

Patton sat up a little straighter, his attention sharpening a bit. "What sort of evidence? Henson's report says the incident was cut-and-dried. No questions on his end. I haven't seen the autopsy report yet—they're a little backed up over at the morgue—but the M.E. didn't mention expecting anything unusual, according to Henson's notes."

She nodded. He was right on all counts. Henson hadn't said anything different to her. "I gave him a peculiar…" God, how did she say this? "It looked like some sort of contact lens, except different." Well that surely explained what she meant. Frustration brimmed. "Henson took it to a friend for unofficial analysis," she offered in lieu of a better explanation. "When he called me last night he was wound up about it. He said he was going over to pick the lens up and that he'd be taking it to the state lab this morning. He sounded pretty excited."

Patton's gaze narrowed with keener interest. "Do you know who he was going to see?"

Alex shook her head. "Not a clue. Some computer whiz. Like I said, he sounded excited. I can't see him falling asleep at the wheel when he'd sounded fully alert when we spoke."

Patton glanced at his watch and swore. "I have a meeting." He stood. "Listen, if you think of anything else Henson said that might sound relevant, give me a call." He passed Alex a business card that included his mobile as well as his home number. "I'll let you know as soon as I hear anything about the memorial service."

Alex tucked the card into her bag, thanked him and made her way through the maze of cold metal desks and warm bodies without stopping to chat with anyone. She wanted to get out of here and to some place where she could think. The idea that just yesterday Henson had been hanging out here had her on the verge of hyperventilating.

A detective who looked vaguely familiar almost bowled her over as he bounded past her. Alex felt like slugging him but didn't want the hassle. She needed out of here. She couldn't breathe.

"Patton," she heard the cop who'd been in such a hurry say, "I've got the preliminary on that house explosion on Morningside."

Alex's feet slowed. Maybe it was oxygen deprivation. Morningside? Wasn't that where Henson had said the whiz kid lived? She lingered, wanted to hear the rest of what the detective had to say.

"They found a body, but it was burned so badly it'll take some time to ID it."

Alex told herself she was probably overreacting.

A lot of people lived in Morningside—this explosion could have nothing to do with Henson's friend who lived there. It could be anything from a meth lab to a gas leak.

"You take a ride over there," Patton suggested. "I'll join you after my meeting."

Alex turned around, waited for Patton and the other detective to catch up to her. There was one more thing she had to know. "By the way, where was the scene of Henson's crash?" The paper hadn't given the location.

Patton looked mildly annoyed that she had waylaid him or maybe the exhaustion was making him testy. "Over on I-95 near Hallandale. Why?"

She shrugged. "Just wondered."

Patton eyed her suspiciously. "If you have other information, Jackson, I need to know. He was my partner."

She shook her head. "It's nothing like that." The white lie felt bitter on her tongue. She should just tell him. "I was just curious that's all." But she couldn't. He already didn't really believe her. What was it he'd said? *If you think of anything else Henson said that might sound relevant…?* Until she could make sense of this herself, she was wasting her time trying to clarify it to anyone else.

"See ya around," he muttered.

Watching Patton go, she realized what she had to do next. She had to know why Henson's vehicle had been found way north of where he'd told her he was going. But first she wanted to know if a computer genius had lived in the Morningside residence where the explosion had occurred.

She also wanted to know if the crime scene techs had found the contact lens in Henson's car. Or if they'd found anything at all that suggested the accident wasn't an accident.

She wanted to know a lot. She needed enough to give Patton reason to consider Henson's death suspicious. And since she wasn't a cop, the chances of Patton telling her were slim to none.

But she had her own sources and methods. Patton wouldn't like it if he found out. She'd never let a man stand in her way before. She wasn't about to now. She owed it to Henson to look into this. Patton wasn't taking her seriously. He was preoccupied, she understood that, but he clearly thought what she'd told him was nothing of consequence. Convincing him might just be impossible, but she had to follow through, either way.

She might not be a detective, but she definitely knew her way around the scene of the crime.

All she needed was access.

CHAPTER 4

Alex called her office as she climbed into her 4Runner. Shannon answered on the first ring. Alex waited patiently while she went through her Never-Happened-we-can-make-anything-go-away spiel. "Hey, do me a favor, will ya?"

"I was just about to call you."

Damn. Alex didn't have time to respond to a call right now. Not that she resented plenty of business, but this just wasn't a good time. Looking at it from the other side of the scenario, was there ever a good time to die? Who was she to complain? She made her living off the dead. That put her and morticians in the same boat. No death and dying, no income.

Evicting the idea that she had anything at all in common with anyone she knew who worked behind the authorized personnel doors of a funeral home, she asked, "What's up?"

"There was a strange call for you this morning. Some really odd guy."

A frown scrunched its way across Alex's forehead. She opted not to point out to Shannon that there were a lot of odd guys in a city the size of Miami. "Did this odd man have a name?" She hadn't dated anyone since the freak who got off on peeking whenever she used the bathroom. Surely it wouldn't be him. Alex was pretty certain she'd made herself crystal clear as to how she felt about hearing from him again.

Three whole weeks without a date. Had to be a record. Cutting herself some slack she had to admit she had been busy. People didn't stop dying just because her dating life was in the toilet. Which was, as she'd just noted a few seconds ago, a good thing for business.

"He wouldn't leave his name. It was very strange. He wanted to know if you were here. When I said no, he asked where he could find you. I offered him your cell number but he hung up on me."

Shannon was right, that was a little weird. Alex couldn't think of anyone she'd ticked off lately. "I suppose if it's important he'll call back. Next time, if he's a jerk, hang up on him." Alex started the engine and backed out of the parking slot. Every business had its share of cranks and jerks. "Did Marg ever come in?"

"Eventually," Shannon said covertly. Alex imagined her craning her neck to make sure Marg wasn't listening. She didn't like that Shannon and Alex kept such close tabs on her.

"Keep an eye on her." Alex thought back to how her mom had forgone her usual third-date sex last night. Maybe sweating to the oldies had only put off the inevitable. She and Robert could have rendezvoused this morning. "We may have to stage another intervention."

"Will do. What's the favor you needed?" Shannon asked, returning her attention to the reason for Alex's call.

"How about checking the *Herald* for anything on an explosion over in Morningside. Happened sometime last night."

Another call came in and Shannon promised to get back to her as soon as she took care of the call and checked the paper.

Alex pulled out onto the street, her mind rolling over and over the idea that Henson was dead. She would miss him. There was no way to deny that. She couldn't help wondering now if she'd made a mistake walking away.

"Enough, Alex." What was she doing? Just because the guy was dead she was going all freaky. Henson was not *the one*. No one was the one. She was happy with her life just the way it was. No one was sorrier than her that he was dead, but she had to get past this obsession with what she hadn't said or done.

It was that stupid contact lens. If she hadn't found it and called him about it, maybe he'd still be alive. That was the part that really bothered her. Whether Patton wanted to take what she said seriously or not, there was something to it. The part that really disturbed her was the call she'd gotten from Henson last night. He'd sounded so excited. The guy who did the analysis had to have given him some pretty juicy feedback to get Henson that pumped. And why had he driven toward Hallandale after picking up the analysis? He didn't live in that direction and hadn't mentioned letting anyone else look at the evidence last night. It didn't make sense. Maybe he had intended to let someone else have a look-see. Another cop who kept the same kind of hours he did.

But wouldn't that have been his partner?

She supposed not, since Patton had been at the

hospital welcoming his new daughter into the world. Maybe Henson and his partner hadn't bonded closely enough in the past six months for Henson to share his obsession with all things electronic.

The idea that something was wrong with the scenario just kept nagging at her.

Alex drove, her destination uncertain. She couldn't go to the scene of the explosion in Morningside until Shannon called her back with an exact location. No point in checking out the crash site where Henson's car had been found; the cops had already been over it and the car was in the hands of forensics.

There was just one thing she could do right now.

Go to the morgue.

The concept was a fairly simple one that had only just occurred to her. The old guy who'd blown off half his head had two eyes—or at least he did before he opted to discharge a .45 into his skull. Most folks who chose contacts over eyeglasses wore two. Maybe there was still one attached to the guy's intact eye.

Anticipation fired through her.

Only one way to find out.

It wasn't that she didn't trust the cops to do their

job. She did, usually. But she'd been doing this job long enough to know she didn't have anything to prompt their attention, to make them look beyond the obvious. Cops operated under the rule of probable cause. Unless something at the scene of Henson's crash looked suspicious or some foul play involving his car was discovered, the case would be ruled accidental. End of story.

Henson had been a damned good cop. Not only was he good at his job, he truly cared. That was exactly why he'd chosen to run the contact lens through some preliminary analysis when any other cop would have dismissed it. There really wasn't any reason to suspect the contact lens was anything relevant. It was just weird looking. But, because the lens was so unusual and Henson had a thing for the odd, he had wanted to be sure. That was just the kind of cop he was. Thorough. Dedicated. Maybe even a little hopeful that he'd be the detective who busted some big spy ring or something.

Damn she was going to miss that guy.

The Morgue Bureau was part of an imposing three-building complex nestled amid a couple of lushly landscaped acres on the perimeter of the Uni-

versity of Miami Medical School Center. South
Florida tropical trees, shrubs and bushes indigenous
to the area highlighted the meticulously cared for
landscape.

Inside, the elegant furnishings, potted palms, soft
lighting and smiling receptionist would almost make
one think of a ritzy resort hotel. At least until you
read the mission statement above the front desk:

To provide accurate, timely, dignified, compas-
sionate and professional death investigative services
for the citizens of Miami-Dade County.

That stopped any warm, fuzzy feelings dead in
their tracks.

As far as Alex was concerned the luxurious details
were wasted on most visitors to the Joseph H. Davis
Center for Forensics Pathology considering they were
dead. But, hey, the place looked great. Didn't even
smell like a morgue. Special electronic air filters
erased the unmistakable odors of formaldehyde and
decomposing bodies.

Alex waved to the receptionist but didn't bother
checking in. She'd been here enough times to know
her way around and headed straight for the work
area of an old friend, Cody Feldman, an evidence
courier. If he wasn't in she'd just have to try her luck

with an assistant medical examiner she'd dated a couple of times. But Cody would be far easier to...coax into doing what she wanted. He had a thing for Alex.

A smile stretched across her lips as she recalled the last time they'd gone out. A couple of months ago. Friday night. Dinner and a movie had been on the agenda but they'd never made it out of her house.

What could she say?

Cody was totally cute. Really young with amazing stamina.

He'd been fun.

She pretty much blew him off after a couple more dates. Not that she wouldn't have enjoyed more but he was one of those young guys who got too attached. In every other way he'd been totally unlike Henson. Cody had been a good change for her until, like Henson, he'd started to get clingy. Why did her every thought have to lead back to Henson.

Dammit.

Although they hadn't dated in a while she and Cody were still friends. She ran into him now and again since they frequented the same night spots.

It was good to have friends in all kinds of places. It was also good to know how to use those assets to one's advantage when the cause was right. She felt certain Henson would appreciate her efforts.

Alex poked her head through the open door to his tiny office. "Hey, Cody." At least someone had an office smaller than hers.

He glanced up from his computer, then did a double take. "Alex." A couple of medical journals and an empty foam cup hit the floor as he shot up out of his chair. "What're you doing here?" He blushed. "I mean…"

Her smile made the transition into a full-blown grin. The guy was adorable when he was all embarrassed and looking flustered. Only a man under the age of twenty-five could still do that and look so sweet. "Good to see you, too."

He pushed his desk chair toward her. "Have a seat." Glancing around his cluttered space he couldn't seem to decide what to say next. Inspiration belatedly struck. "You want some coffee? Nancy just made a fresh pot." He hitched his thumb toward the end of the hall where the lounge could be found. "She makes the best." He licked his lips and blinked as if he'd abruptly drawn a big old blank.

Alex shook her head. "No thanks. I'm good." She moved a little farther into his territory, pushing the chair out of her way as she went. "I need to ask a favor," she offered humbly.

He opened his arms wide. "Sure. Anything."

His face had gone from pink to red. Alex was pretty sure he'd just remembered one night in particular when she'd made him beg for mercy.

That was the thing about being a mature woman and dating a younger guy. They were so easily amused.

Alex took a moment to appreciate her friend's casually sexy appearance. His trousers were navy, one of her favorite colors, his shirt was striped in a paler blue, yellow and green. The shirttail was untucked on one side. Not a fashion statement, simply a result of his slightly nerdish predisposition. The brown loafers were polished. His face clean shaven. His dark hair tousled and his gray eyes clear and bright. Maybe they'd go out again sometime, when he'd gotten over the whole I-want-to-be-with-you-forever syndrome.

"You got a stiff last night—"

His eyes suddenly widened and his face paled as if he'd been caught doing something that would get him seriously grounded.

Alex laughed softly. "Not that kind of stiff, Cody, the other kind." She'd been hanging around with too many cops and was picking up all their slang.

"Oh." The pink started to creep up from his collar again. "We got five last night."

She nodded. "Detective Rich Henson worked this case. Caucasian, in his late fifties or early sixties, took a .45 to his head."

"Yeah." Recognition flared in his expression. "I imagine that was a real mess."

She shook her head. "I'll never understand why these guys don't consider the mess they're going to leave when they opt for the suicide route."

Cody was nodding in agreement.

"You think it'd be a problem if I took another look at the body?"

A flicker of hesitation had her hastily adding, "The guy doesn't have any family. And the cops have pretty much closed the case. There's just something I'm curious about."

Still looking a little unsure, he said, "He's scheduled for the full treatment tomorrow morning. Letting you look at him wouldn't really be—"

He was on the verge of saying no. "I swear I won't do anything that'll get you in trouble. I just need to check one little thing." She held her breath, then quickly added in hopes of alleviating any final reservations he might have, "It's not like I haven't already seen him." The full treatment was a no holds barred complete autopsy. Everyone got the full treatment unless the family requested otherwise.

He checked his watch. "I don't guess there'd be any harm. Like you said you've already seen him…been in the same room with him." Their eyes locked. "Just let me make sure the cooler is…ah…clear."

"I really appreciate it." She gave him her best you're-my-hero look of gratitude.

"I'll be back in thirty seconds," he promised as he backed out of his office.

She couldn't be certain whether he backed out because he was afraid she'd follow him or if he feared she'd disappear before he got back. A quick peek out the door confirmed her conclusion that he would probably run the whole distance to the cooler.

Leaning against the door frame to watch for his return she couldn't help thinking that men were like puppies—she adored them but she didn't want to have to clean up after one on a regular basis. She liked her total independence. She didn't have to answer to anyone. How many women her age could say that? How many others looked back on their lives and considered all they would change if given the opportunity.

Not Alex. She wouldn't change a thing. Sure, being alone hadn't always been rosy, but she felt completely satisfied with who she was, where she'd been and where she was going. That was an accomplishment in and of itself.

That big ol' grin Henson liked to flash at her popped into her head and suddenly she didn't feel so sure of all she'd just affirmed. She blinked away the image. She had to be hormonal. She never had this much trouble with self-doubt.

True to his word, Cody was back in about half a minute. "This way." He gestured in the direction from which he'd just returned.

Alex let him lead the way though she knew the route. The few times she'd visited had been when she'd been dating another member of the esteemed staff. Way before Cody's time.

Cody checked the log sheet and headed for the drawer where Charlie Crane awaited two things, an autopsy and then for the state to claim his body since there was no next of kin. En route her guide pointed to a box of latex gloves stationed on a counter. Alex had them in place before Cody had rested his hand on the pull of the cooler drawer.

With one last fleeting look at the door, he lugged

the drawer open. As if having second thoughts, he hesitated before lowering the zipper on the body bag. "Make it quick, okay? And be really careful not to...well, you know."

"Don't worry."

He opened the bag that helped to keep the body fresh while in a refrigerated state.

With the old guy's upper torso and what was left of his head fully exposed to her, Cody backed away. "I'll keep watch outside."

She nodded and he left her to her business.

It wasn't that Alex got any kind of thrill out of touching a dead guy, but this had to be done.

Working quickly, she first surveyed what was left of his head. His body was nude so anything he'd had in his pockets would be beyond her reach at this point. It would take an act of congress or proof of kinship to get her hands on his personal effects.

The right eye remained intact and exactly where it should be in its socket.

"Okay, Charlie," she murmured. "Let's have a look."

Gingerly, she lifted the eyelid and surveyed the eyeball. She shuddered, couldn't help herself. The body changed drastically after twenty-four hours without blood flowing through the veins. The skin looked gray with the slightest marbling effect deep beneath the surface. The eyes were cloudy, the pupils fully dilated. The flesh was cold—that was the worst. Nothing smelled as creepy as chilled flesh. Her stomach knotted.

Kicking aside her squeamishness, she touched the eyeball, sliding the pad of her finger over it. Nothing. Frowning, she checked again just to be sure.

If he'd been wearing a second lens, it was gone now.

"Dammit."

She zipped the bag carefully over what was left of Charlie Crane and closed the drawer. For a moment she just stood there, feeling sad for him. No one should die alone.

Henson had died alone.

The idea that she might very well die that way made her stomach spasm all over again. Of course there was always the chance her mother would outlive her. But what if she didn't?

Would she end up in the morgue with no family to claim her?

Nah. Shannon would claim her. See that she got a proper funeral. At least as long as she was still alive.

Despite her chosen career field, this was the first

time Alex could recall consciously considering what would happen to her when she died. Other than the usual decomposition, that is.

This whole thing with Henson had really shaken her up.

Alex peeled off the gloves and disposed of them as she crossed the room. She opened the door and Cody whipped around with a start.

"Finished?"

He tried to look calm and composed but he didn't fool her. He'd been sweating every second of the six or seven minutes she'd been in there.

"Yeah. Thanks, man, I owe you."

Between that announcement and the whoosh of the door closing behind her, he relaxed. Looked downright ready to melt into a puddle of equal parts physical need and mental relief.

"We could have dinner," he suggested tentatively.

Alex hooked her arm in his and headed toward his office. "We could."

"Name the night." He was feeling cockier now, grinning like a kid looking forward to Christmas.

Oh, yes, easily amused.

She went on tiptoe and placed a chaste kiss on his cheek. "I'll call you."

Giving him a show he wouldn't soon forget, she strutted away. She didn't have to look back to know he'd enjoyed every second of it.

Men were so predictable.

God love 'em.

The driveway was empty when Alex arrived at the house Charlie Crane had called home until he'd elected to end his existence. She scanned the neighborhood as she pulled on a pair of latex gloves. At half past ten in the morning most folks were either at work or on the beach. The morning was far too glorious to spend cooped up inside unless you were physically unable to get out and around.

Alex was banking on the idea that the landlord hadn't gotten around to taking care of the broken lock on Charlie's apartment after the first cops on the scene had basically kicked in the door.

And she was right. The door opened with a simple twist of the knob. The splintered wood on the interior side of the casing confirmed that the repairman hadn't gotten around to the job yet. It wasn't as if the landlord really cared. The stuff inside didn't belong to him and this was one of the safest neighborhoods in the city. Break-ins and vandalism rarely occurred.

After pushing the door shut behind her, she flipped on the overhead lights. The front door opened into the nondescript living room with its renter's white walls and builder's grade carpeting in the ever-popular sand color. A hall beyond the living room took her deeper into the house. She flipped on more lights as she went. It was broad daylight outside but the shuttered windows left the place in heavy shadows. The rest of the house was comprised of a kitchen, bathroom and three bedrooms, one of which had been turned into a den, complete with wood paneling.

She searched the den first. She doubted she'd missed anything but she was here, might as well take a second look. Each drawer, shelf and niche. Nothing but magazines, papers and pens.

Before moving on to the bathroom and bedrooms, she took a moment to riffle through the papers. She didn't really expect to find anything. The likelihood of her recognizing something that shouldn't be there was pretty low. Again, what the hell? Might as well check it out since she was here.

Utility receipts. Rent receipts. Not much else to speak of outside the usual credit card invitations.

The bathroom offered no better. Mouthwash,

toothpaste, deodorant. No prescription medications, not even a bottle of aspirin.

The idea of a man who'd blown off the better portion of his head not having a bottle of aspirin in the house gave her pause. Everyone got headaches. She took a mental step back and looked at the room again.

This time she nailed what felt wrong.

The soap rest in the shower-tub combination was clean. No soap residue, nothing. She dragged the shower curtain back to be sure she hadn't missed a bottle of liquid body wash. Not even a ring around the tub. No soap scum whatsoever.

Anticipation buzzing, she checked under the sink next. Clean as a whistle.

The narrow linen closet next to the vanity was stocked with half a dozen or so towels and an equal number of washcloths. All in white. She picked them up one at a time and sniffed, felt the texture of the terry cloth. Unwashed. Unused.

Her pulse raced as she moved to the bedrooms. Clothes hung in the closet. All new. No price tags, but she could tell. The fabrics had never been worn much less laundered.

The dresser drawers rendered the same. Nice, neatly stored, *new* underclothes, including socks. She went to the kitchen next. The cabinets were well stocked with a variety of canned goods, dishes and cookware. All spotless and mirror shiny. No way anyone had prepared or consumed a meal using any of it.

The fridge was stocked, as well. None of the goods inside had been opened. Not the milk, not the cheese and bologna. Not a single item.

All brand-new.

Next to the rear entrance was a set of bifold louvered doors that concealed the place where a washer and dryer would be. Dust was the only thing she discovered there. No detergent. No cleaning supplies for taking care of the rest of the house.

The second bedroom was devoid of signs of occupancy as the laundry closet had been.

According to the landlord Charlie Crane had rented this place a year ago. Why hadn't he lived here? And why the fresh foods in the fridge?

That creepy sensation danced up her spine again. She shook it off and headed back to the den, the only place where she'd found anything that wasn't practically sterile.

She got out all the receipts and studied them. They told her nothing. None had Crane's signature. The address labels on the magazines sported his name and address but not one appeared to have been perused. No wrinkled or dog-eared pages.

This time she took the drawers out of the desk and checked the bottoms the way she'd seen it done in the movies. Unlike the protagonists on the big screen, she came up empty-handed.

She sat back on her haunches, surrounded by the drawers she'd dragged from the desk. What was the deal with this guy? This was weird. Just like the damned contact lens he'd been wearing.

Nelly's voice shattered the silence and her heart surged into her throat.

"Shit." She caught her breath and reached into her pants pocket for her phone. Damn thing about gave her a heart attack.

"I've got that address for you."

Shannon. Alex had almost forgotten. She drew in a deep, calming breath. "Great."

The address wasn't in the swanky historic district of Morningside but it was no shabby location, either.

"Thanks, Shannon. I'm headed that way."

"You wanna tell me what's going on?"

Alex finished shoving the last of the drawers back into place, holding the phone with her shoulder. "I'm not sure yet. I'll catch up with you later." She closed her phone and tucked it back into her pocket before her friend could argue. Shannon knew her too well. She would have kept asking questions until she had some answers. Alex didn't have the right answers yet. Maybe there weren't any.

But she intended to find out.

Something about this old guy's death got Henson killed. The idea that her turning that contact lens over to him might have been the reason he was dead, wouldn't be banished from her mind.

She had to know for sure.

Nothing she'd found in this house would have alerted the police. Cops didn't go around sniffing towels and checking soap dishes unless they had probable cause. This was Miami, for Christ's sake, they got all the probable cause they could handle without going out of their way to look for it. Henson wouldn't have looked at anything like this unless something specific in the house had stood out to him or the autopsy report gave reason to suspect suicide wasn't the cause of death. Hell, she wouldn't have come here this morning if not for the contact lens and Henson's death. There was nothing, except that damned weird lens and even it might be nothing.

But she couldn't stop until she was sure.

The sun had started to heat up big-time when she went outside again. What she'd found in the house had spooked her and she didn't like the feeling.

However bizarre the situation got, she intended to follow it through. Once she'd figured out if the explosion was connected to Crane and her friend, she would go back to Henson's partner and dump the whole theory in his lap. He could laugh at her if he wanted to, but she had to do what she had to do.

She'd reached to open the driver's side door of her 4Runner when the creeps performed its spine-chilling tap dance for the second time since she'd arrived.

Turning slowly she took a long, hard look around her. The driveways along the street were still empty. The houses, the whole neighborhood for that matter, were quiet. If anyone was home it was impossible to tell.

Still, she recognized the sensation. Knew it all too well from a couple of jerks she'd dated before her *jerkdar* had kicked in fully at age twenty.

Someone was watching her.

Nothing in this world pissed her off more than the idea of someone playing the intimidation game. Just to make sure she got her point across to whomever might be scrutinizing her, she gave a little wave using one particular finger that announced how she felt loudly and clearly.

She climbed into her SUV and backed out onto the street. After a thorough check of her mirrors, she headed toward Morningside to find out who'd been killed last night.

Who knew? Maybe there was a job in it. At any rate, she could leave her card to cover for her uninvited appearance.

CHAPTER 5

What remained of the house in Morningside, just east of Biscayne Boulevard, a few blocks from the bay was indicative of typical Florida construction. One level, painted a pale pink with shutters in a deeper pink shade. The slightly overgrown yard was bordered by a hibiscus hedge and a strand of yellow crime scene tape that flopped in the sporadic breeze.

A team of forensics techs was rummaging through the wreckage. She recognized one of the detectives who emerged from his car and crossed the yard to survey the ongoing work. The guy who'd almost knocked her down getting word to Detective Patton about the body that had been recovered from this gruesome scene.

No way was she going to get across that line. The detective hadn't appeared friendly at the station, and she doubted his disposition would improve in the field. She didn't really need to get that close, she supposed. If the contact lens was in the house there definitely wasn't anything left of it now.

What she needed was to confirm who had lived here.

Alex drove farther down the block and parked at the curb. At one point in her varied career, when she had been around twenty-one, she'd briefly sold vacuum cleaners door to door. Electrolux. No home should be without one had been her motto. Just another one of her early careers that hadn't lasted. Maybe it was her impatience with the extreme pressure to meet a certain quota. How was she supposed to talk people into buying something if they didn't, *a*, need it, or, *b*, want it? Then there were the folks who slammed the door in her face or the ones who were just plain rude.

That was the nice thing about cleaning up after the dead, the dead didn't talk back or argue or any of that stuff.

She climbed out of her 4Runner and headed to door number one, an older ranch-style home that had obviously been remodeled to fit in with the escalating value of the property north of downtown Miami.

Three rings of the doorbell later and a young woman, twenty-five maybe, opened the door far enough to check out Alex. "Yes?" she asked tentatively.

Judging by the terry cloth fabric, she was still in her robe. The abrupt sound of screaming behind her signaled at least one toddler was likely vying for her attention even as she continued to scrutinize Alex.

"I apologize for the intrusion, ma'am, but I'd like to ask you a few questions about the explosion last night."

Uncertainty flickered in her brown eyes. "Are you the police?"

"The detective and the forensics techs are digging through the rubble now," Alex dodged. "My job is to find out if any of the neighbors saw or heard anything unusual before the event."

She hoped like hell the woman would accept that as a yes. Lying by omission appeared to be a steady appointment on her agenda today.

"I answered the officer's questions last night," she said, seemingly to herself. She heaved a sigh at another bout of ranting behind her. "Give me just a moment and I'll be with you."

The door closed and Alex heard the woman fussing at the children. Deciding she needed to look the part, Alex dug a small notepad and pen from her bag. When the fretting had quieted, the door opened once more. Leaving it open a crack, the woman stepped out onto the stoop with Alex.

"I really don't know anything useful," she started off. "We go to bed early around here. I heard the explosion, of course." She paused, her gaze expectant as if she didn't know what to say next.

Alex nodded. "What can you tell me about the residents?"

"Timothy O'Neill lives—" she cleared her throat "—lived there alone." She stared in the direction of the damaged house. "He leased it from the owners when they moved into the retirement center nearby."

"I see," Alex said, nodding agreeably.

"Thank God Mrs. Baker was visiting with her sister in Tampa. Mrs. Baker lives in the house right next door. I'm sure the explosion would have scared her to death."

"What can you tell me about Timothy?" Alex prodded. That was what she really wanted to know. She didn't need to know who his neighbors were.

The woman shrugged. "I hate to speak ill of the dead, but he was a little strange, if you know what I mean."

Alex scribbled a couple of words just to make herself look credible.

"I didn't mention this to the officer last night because I was too stunned, but Timothy was sort of…you know, a geek…or nerd."

More scribbling. "Really?"

Uncertainty flashed in her eyes again. "Maybe I shouldn't—"

"Please," Alex urged, "this may prove very useful."

The woman's gaze wandered toward the devastation once more. "He didn't get out much. Spent all his time piddling around with computers." She leaned closer as if what she had to say next was top secret. "Mrs. Baker went over once when Timothy was first moving in. You know, checking out the new neighbor to make sure he wasn't an ax murderer or anything. She said the basement was packed with all sorts of electronic gadgets. At least half a dozen computers. She said it was bizarre. Like something from a science fiction movie."

Alex's heart rate reacted to an adrenaline dump. "Is that what Timothy did for a living?"

She nodded. "My husband says he's supposedly a genius or something when it comes to computers and cyberspace." She cleared her throat again. "Was supposed to be, I should say. But he was a real recluse. Hardly ever came out of the house."

No wonder Henson didn't talk about the guy to his friends, that was probably part of their arrangement. A kid that reclusive wouldn't want any attention.

The sound of something crashing inside the house ended the discussion. Alex thanked her and moved on to the next house.

After hearing the same story from three neighbors, Alex felt confident that Timothy O'Neill was the unofficial expert Henson had visited last night.

She decided to pull over at the scene and try her luck with Detective Dickhead. Maybe he'd give something away. She needed to be sure Timothy O'Neill was dead. His neighbors assumed he was since they had seen the M.E. take a body from the house.

The detective she'd noticed at the scene now leaned against his car speaking to someone on his mobile phone. Alex parked behind him and got out of her SUV. He glanced her way but didn't bother waving.

It was then, something about the way he noted her arrival with a dismissive glance, that recognition flared. She knew this guy.

He'd been the detective on the case when Patsy's Clip Joint had been burglarized. It sounded weird, she knew, but there were people who would break into any place. Fortunately none of the animals had been taken. Just a few dollars in cash and a large metal cage. Alex had her own ideas as to why the cage had been taken.

But this detective. She glared at him. Detective Daryl Winston. He'd been a real jerk to Patsy. Alex had seen him from across the alley, but hadn't known until later how he'd talked down to Patsy.

She despised guys like him.

Alex walked toward the house, hadn't even reached the crime scene tape when he shouted, "Where do you think you're going?"

Well at least she had his attention now. She turned around and flashed him a smile. "I'm Alex Jackson. Never Happened. I thought I'd leave my card for the owner." She snagged a card from her bag and waved it at him.

The idea of her getting a job here wasn't exactly plausible considering the house would need a bulldozer a whole lot more than it would need her. But, hey, it was a conversation starter.

"I know who you are." Still reclined against his car, he smirked, then executed a long perusal of her from head to toe. "Get real, Jackson, unless you've branched out into rubble removal, this is way out of your league."

"Who was the crispy critter?" she asked, getting down on his level as she walked toward him. Crispy critter was cop speak for a burned-beyond-recognition victim. She winced inwardly at the seemingly heartless moniker.

"No comment."

"Come on, I know the M.E. removed a body. Timothy O'Neill?"

Winston crossed his arms over his chest and eyed her suspiciously. "You know I can't discuss the details of a case with you."

"The news has already reported it." One of the neighbors had told her that she'd heard the details on the radio earlier that morning.

"Well, then why ya asking?" Another one of those smirks made Alex want to slap him cross-eyed.

"Maybe I'm curious, Winston. Is that a crime?" She matched his stance, careful to prop her arms under her breasts for full enhancement.

His gaze strayed to her cleavage. "I suppose not. It's O'Neill's house. He was found in the basement with all his computer equipment or what was left of it. It's probably him, but we don't have an official confirmation yet. The press is guessing the same as we are at this point."

"I suppose he'll be identified by dental records?" That was the most commonly used method and the quickest.

"The lower jaw is intact and that's about all." He shook his head and let go a heavy breath. "But, unfortunately, we haven't been able to track down a dentist who had him as a patient. His family insists he never went to a dentist as a child. So it's way too early to say anything for sure."

Damn. "That's too bad." That meant no burying the body, no closure, until the remains had been officially ID'd. "Any idea what caused the explosion?"

"We're still working on that." He checked out her boobs once more. "Besides, you know I couldn't give you anything about those details. We still have to determine if it was accidental or if foul play was involved."

"Right." She tucked her hands into her back pockets. "See ya around, Winston."

"Yeah." His mobile rang.

Alex slid behind the wheel of her car and stared at what used to be Timothy O'Neill's home. There was no doubt in her mind that this was the place Henson had brought the contact lens.

Her stomach cramped.

Henson had called her, excited that the analysis had confirmed the lens was more than met the eye— no pun intended. Now Henson was dead. His friend who'd done the analysis was dead.

All because of the contact lens she'd found. With either Henson or O'Neill abruptly dying she could call it a fluke, but with both, no way it was a mere coincidence.

What did she do about that?

How did she make Patton believe that this explosion had something to do with Henson's accident— that it probably wasn't an accident?

She had no proof. Nothing.

The story sounded melodramatic even to her. But she couldn't just pretend it never happened. She owed it to Henson, it was the least she could do. She had to see this through whether the police believed her or not.

Banging on the window next to her made her jump. Three seconds passed before Alex's heart slid back down into her throat and started to beat again.

She lowered her window and glared at Winston. "What?" He'd scared the hell of her.

He grinned like a jackass. "Thought I'd let you

know that I'd just gotten a call about a possible homicide scene not too far from here. I can give you the address if you want to run over there and see if there's any work to be drummed up."

She didn't give him the finger, which had been her first inclination. Instead she smiled, pulled the gear shift into Reverse and rolled away from him. He was still laughing when she glanced into her rearview mirror after turning around and driving away.

Asshole.

Alex drove back to the office. As usual, her parking spot was taken. She squeezed into an open space between a Cadillac and a Honda.

"Got a call." Shannon was waving a message at her as she walked through the door. Alex wondered vaguely whatever happened to "Hello, how has your morning been?"

She snagged the message. "Thanks. Where's Marg?" The lounge door was wide open and from her position in front of Shannon's desk Alex could see that the room was empty. This wasn't a good sign.

"She left less than an hour after she got here and never came back." Shannon shrugged, then pointed to the message in Alex's hand. "They're in kind of a hurry. Wanted to know if you could come right over. I was about to call you."

Alex read over the message. Apartment building over in Carol City. She knew the place. "What's the rush?" Not that she didn't understand the need to get a cleanup done, considering the most plausible source of the problem, but hurrying wouldn't change the fact that someone was most likely deceased.

"The guy lived on the second floor. Apparently he's been dead for almost two weeks without anyone missing him. He might not have been missed at all if his downstairs neighbor hadn't noticed something oozing from her kitchen ceiling."

Ugh. Her favorite kind of duty. "I'm on my way," Alex mumbled with about as much enthusiasm as a prisoner on his final walk toward execution.

She popped into the bathroom and took care of business, pulled her hair up into a ponytail and stared at her reflection, wondering what Fate had against her. She was reasonably intelligent and attractive, why was it that her primary skill appeared to be cleaning up after the dead? Somebody had to do it. That was her stock answer whenever she felt sorry for herself.

Maybe that was the reason her life had not taken

the usual journey. Never had a husband. No kids. No serious relationships. But that was what she'd wanted? Wasn't it?

She thought about Henson and what he'd wanted, a long-term relationship…a commitment. What if she'd chosen that path? What if she'd taken the chance…?

She would have been sorry. Henson would still be dead and she would be…left with all the emotional baggage.

That was precisely why she never went there. No risk, no regret.

"Damn straight," she growled at the uncertainty she saw in her eyes.

She never second-guessed herself like this. Evidently the recent rash of deaths involving people who basically lived alone or had no one who looked in on them had gotten under her skin. Yeah, right. If only it were that simple. It was Henson. Dammit.

Shaking off the annoying sentiments, she headed for Carol City. The sooner she dived into the apartment's cleanup, the sooner she'd be done.

The building's super led her to the first-floor apartment where the neighbor had discovered the leak in her ceiling. The fluids had seeped through the ceiling and oozed down the wall next to her kitchen table. She'd refused to return to the apartment until it was cleaned up and repainted.

No problem for Alex. She'd have this place tiptop in no time.

The apartment on the second floor was a different story. The moment the super opened the door, the stench assaulted Alex's olfactory nerves. Decaying flesh and dissipating putrid gases were never pleasant smells. The tenant had been dead, according to what the M.E.'s office had told the super, at least twelve days. He'd died in his kitchen, lying on the floor, directly above the kitchen on the first level.

Twelve days. That was more than enough time for things to get ugly. Immediately after death the body temperature started to drop, and rigor mortis began, only to reverse itself about two days later. After nearly a couple of weeks putrefaction had already taken place and things were pretty much flat and creamy. The body fluids that had escaped had seeped into everything, including the kitchen downstairs.

Alex donned her hazmat jumpsuit, gloves, et cetera, and went to work, cleaning not only every surface involved but also the air. The gases released by decomposing body fluids, such as spinal fluid, could be extremely toxic. The better part of the day passed before she was packed up and ready to go. The super planned to do the painting himself, which was fine by her.

She loaded the hazmat bags containing the remains she would need to dispose of into the cargo area of her 4Runner. The jumpsuit, gloves and shoe covers she'd worn were bagged and ready to dump, as well.

Her work was done.

It wasn't that late. She should probably go back by the office after she'd taken care of disposal. Or maybe she'd go talk to Henson's partner again and broach the subject of the contact lens and the house over in Morningside.

All she could do was try to convince him that something very wrong had gone down last night.

"Alex Jackson?"

Alex almost ran off the causeway at the sound of the male voice coming from her backseat.

Her fingers went automatically to the console and the pepper spray she kept there.

"Whoever the hell you are," she warned, "this stuff is potent. I'm going to pull over." She was already slowing, simultaneously moving toward the emergency lane. "And you'd better get the hell outta here as soon as I stop or you'll regret it."

"Wait! Please. I'm sorry if I scared you."

She relaxed marginally. Okay, what kind of robber, rapist or killer apologized?

"Who are you?" Though she'd eased off the brake and shifted her foot back to the accelerator, she kept her hand on her weapon.

He cleared his throat. "I'm going to sit up now. Don't freak out, okay?"

She glanced at her rearview mirror. "Okay." What was he, a leper or something? He'd apologized for scaring her when he was the one who sounded terrified. Not to mention he'd prepared her for whatever she would see when he sat up. What kind of bad guy went to all that trouble?

Green eyes, sandy blond hair appeared in her mirror. Young. Twenty-something, she guessed.

"Who are you?" she asked again, her fight defenses still firmly in place.

"My name is Timothy O'Neill."

Her surprise had her weaving into the left lane much to the dismay of the other drivers on the street. Horns blasted.

She let go of the spray can and allowed her right

hand to rejoin her left on the steering wheel. At least she knew now why he'd warned her not to freak out.

Her first thought was to ask why he'd been hiding in her car. Second was…hell, she didn't know what. But there was one point she had to raise. "I thought you were dead."

What the hell was she supposed to do with him? Take him to the police? How had he found her? More importantly, why?

"I'm supposed to be," he said quietly. He looked away when she would have made eye contact with him again.

"It was a buddy of mine. Back at my house. He was pirating movies and—"

He abruptly shut up.

"Don't worry," she encouraged, "whatever your friend was doing doesn't make any difference now."

His jaw worked futilely a couple of times before anything actually came out. "Anyway, last night I was upstairs getting something to eat. I saw Detective Henson's car pull into the drive. I mean—" he cleared his throat again "—I didn't really see his car. It was dark. I saw the headlights, but I knew it was him. I was expecting him. But when he came in he wasn't alone."

"His partner was with him?" She felt certain that wasn't the case, but she needed to ask. She didn't know Patton that well, but he was one of the good guys. Henson had said as much plenty of times.

"I didn't see the guy but I heard his voice." He shrank back into the rear seat, looking like a small boy rather than a grown man. "I don't think this was his partner. Detective Henson was saying stuff like *You won't get away with this* and *Leave the kid alone, he was just doing me a favor.*"

A keen sense of anticipation zinged through Alex. She'd been right. Timothy O'Neill was the guy Henson had visited last night. And apparently Henson had met with someone else on his way to Timothy's house. Why hadn't he mentioned that to her? Her breath hitched. He'd said he was getting another call before he said good-night. Could that caller have been the man who killed him?

Henson hadn't been alone. The guy with him had to be the caller, someone he'd rendezvoused with *after* talking to Alex. Goose bumps spilled over her skin. "What did you do, Timothy?"

He was staring out the passenger side window now. "I knew the kid Henson was talking about was me. He always called me *kid.*" His voice sounded distant. "So

I hid. I didn't think. I just reacted. I hid in the pantry. Henson and the dude with him went down to the basement. I could hear all this shouting…."

Ten seconds passed before he spoke again. Alex's heart pounded three times for each one.

"I just froze. I couldn't move. Couldn't call out for help. Not that it would have done any good."

Alex kept quiet. Let him continue in his own time. She picked up some speed, eased more fully into the flow of traffic on the causeway and tried to focus on driving. Back to her office? Home? She couldn't decide so she just drove.

"There was a lot of noise."

Alex met his eyes in the mirror but he wasn't looking at her. He was remembering.

"I figured the guy was tearing up my lab. I could hear Lenny. My friend," he explained. "He was yelling that he didn't know what the guy was talking about. Henson was saying something, but I couldn't make out his words. I knew…" Alex glanced up again, this time his gaze collided with hers in the mirror. "I knew we were all going to die."

But he hadn't…obviously.

"What did you do then?" she prompted quietly when he remained silent for more miles than she could bear.

"I got out. Ran. Tried to wake one of my neighbors so I could call the police but no one was home. Or they were in bed." He scrubbed a hand over his pale face. "I made my way back to my house, would have gone back inside to try to stop whatever the hell was going on, but Henson and the guy came out."

"Did you see the guy's face this time?" Adrenaline did a number on her pulse rate. This could prove Henson's accident was no accident.

"No." The croaked word was barely audible. "It was dark and I couldn't see from where I was hidden in the shrubs next door." He released a shuddering breath. "When they'd driven away...I was going to go back and check on my friend...." He blinked. "And the house exploded right in front of me."

Poor guy. Damn.

"You okay?"

He didn't answer for a moment. Then the idea that she was talking to him kicked in. "Yeah... sure...I'm okay."

"We should go to the police." Fury burned through her. The guy he'd left with had no doubt forced him to drive to the very place he would die that night. His accident hadn't been an accident at all. Someone had killed Henson. Someone who had something to do with Charlie Crane's death and that damned contact lens.

"No way." Timothy sat forward. "Just let me out here. I'm not going to the police. Whoever the hell that guy was, he wanted just one thing. I'm not getting involved with this. No way. It's too dangerous."

He scooted to the passenger-side door.

Alex divided her attention between him and the traffic all around her. She had to calm him down. "Let me take you to my place. You'll be safe there."

"You don't get it." He looked ready to jump out the door with her moving at fifty-five miles per hour across the causeway. "This thing you gave Henson is like poison. Anyone who touches it is going to end up dead."

Shifting her full attention back to traffic she tamped down the natural trepidation his words evoked. "What exactly is it?"

"Some kind of new technology storage device, works just like a computer only it's tiny and somehow the brain issues commands through the optic nerve. I've heard rumors about that kind of stuff but I had no idea it existed yet. That thing has a shitload of classified information on it. Most of it's encrypted."

"What kind of classified information?" She'd

made up her mind. They were going to the cops. If she could keep him distracted long enough he might not even notice until they were there already.

"Government stuff. The kind of stuff we civilians aren't supposed to see if we want to stay alive."

Government? Classified? She thought about Charlie Crane. He hadn't exactly looked like the James Bond type. But then again, she'd never known a real-life spy.

"Let me out at the next light."

"Look, Timothy." She sped through the amber light instead of slowing for the stop, afraid he'd make a run for it. She needed him. Without this guy Patton would never believe her. "We really need to go to the cops."

He moved up close behind her seat again. "I just wanted to warn you. I figured you deserved a chance to save yourself since Henson liked you so much."

Her chest tightened. "If we don't go to the police they won't be able to find his killer."

"I have to stay dead." Their gazes locked in the rearview mirror once more. "It's the only chance I've got of staying alive." He reached past her seat and placed a small plastic sandwich bag on her console. "I'd get rid of that thing if I were you."

She didn't have to look to know it was the lens she'd given to Henson. "You had it on you when Henson and the killer arrived?"

He nodded. "It was too important to leave in the lab with my friend."

His dead friend.

Damn. This was even worse that she'd suspected.

"Make the next right," he instructed. "I have to disappear for a while."

Alex took the turn and found a place along the street to park. A quick check of her mirrors confirmed that she hadn't been followed.

"Do you have a car?" If walking was his plan for disappearing, he needed to rethink his strategy.

"I have transportation," he told her without telling her anything at all. "Like I said, I would have disappeared already but I needed to warn you."

"I appreciate that." What next? She had to convince him that going to the police was the only reasonable option.

"I don't know what he might have gotten out of Henson before he killed him," Timothy cautioned, "but I wouldn't take any chances. You should disappear, Alex. Or you could end up dead, too."

Jesus, she hadn't even thought of that. What if

Henson told that guy that she'd seen the contact lens? Would it matter? No. She was certain Henson wouldn't have done anything to endanger her. No way. He would have died first.

Emotion swelled in her throat.

"Timothy," she countered with as much determination as she could muster, "we have to talk to Henson's partner."

"You don't get it," he snapped, "if they know I'm still alive, if they figure out I've contacted you, we're both dead." He reached for the door handle. "I've done all I can do."

CHAPTER 6

Alex sat on her closed toilet lid and stared at the contact lens, storage device, whatever the hell it was that Timothy O'Neill had given back to her. It was hard, like a small piece of glass or firm plastic. Nothing like the usual sort of contact lens.

The words *government, classified, encrypted* kept whirling in her thoughts, getting all mixed up with the idea that this tiny gadget had gotten her friend as well as at least one other person killed.

And it was her fault.

If she hadn't found it.

If she'd just tossed the damned eyeball.

But she hadn't. She'd done her job and now Henson was dead. The worst part was that no one seemed to be aware of how and why he'd died. To say no one cared would be wrong. Henson had too many friends, including his partner. But no one had ruled out the whole "accident" assumption.

She stared at the telephone receiver she'd been clutching in her hand since she'd come into the bathroom. Doing nothing was wrong. She had to do something. Holding her breath, she turned the receiver button side up and entered Patton's number. She knew it by heart after more than an hour of sitting here trying to decide if she should call him or not.

Most likely he'd think she was crazy, but she had to do this for Henson. He deserved justice, by God.

Jimmy Patton answered after only the second ring.

"This is Alex Jackson."

She didn't actually have to bother with her full name, most of the homicide detectives knew her, but she'd felt the need to make this sound official.

"What's up, Jackson? Oh damn. I was supposed to call you about the memorial service. It's been crazy all day. I'm just now getting away. Gotta get back to the hospital and see my wife and baby girl."

Alex could hear the pride in his voice as well as the traffic sounds in the background. Patton was apparently on his way home. He drove a convertible T-Bird, kept the top down all year round he was so damned proud of it. She wondered if that would change now that he was a father. He'd probably convert to a minivan the moment he saw how uncool a car seat looked in the backseat of his T-Bird.

She swallowed, steadied her voice and took the plunge. "Anything new on Henson's accident?"

Silence.

Could he possibly already know foul play was involved? Would he find her question suspicious? After all, she was one of the last people to talk to Henson last night.

"What was that?" he asked. "You cut out there for a sec."

Wetting her lips, she tried her best not to let her voice reverberate with the tension gripping her throat. "Did you determine if Henson's accident was an…accident?"

"That's what it looks like so far. No reason to suspect otherwise. We're still waiting for a couple more reports." He hesitated. "What's going on, Jackson? Why do you sound so nervous?"

Damn. Alex cringed. "What was the time and location of that memorial service?" She hoped like hell the abrupt question would derail his suspicion.

"Tomorrow, two-thirty. St. Mary's over on Second Avenue. The family'll conduct a private funeral later, after the autopsy."

What did she say now? "Thanks. I…just can't believe he's gone."

Patton made a knowing sound in his throat. "Had you and Henson…you know…thought of getting back together?" He chuckled good-naturedly. "I knew he still had a thing for you."

Would he tell her more if he thought she and Henson were involved again?

She wasn't about to lie like that about a friend, especially a dead one.

"No, we were just friends," she confessed. "I guess I'm stunned that he's gone. That's all. He sounded fine to me last night and then I wake up this morning to hear he's dead."

"Look, Jackson," Patton said, his voice somber. "We all look for some way to explain an unexpected death like this. Henson was a top-notch detective and a great friend. He'll be sorely missed. If there was anything at all besides Fate that played a hand in his death, I'll find it. You don't need to worry about that."

She didn't doubt his sincerity, but was sincerity enough? Could she convince Patton of what she suspected without the benefit of Timothy O'Neill to back her up? If she did tell him everything and passed this thing—she glared at the plastic bag—on to him, would his life be in danger, as well? But then, he was a cop, danger was part of the job.

What about his wife and child?

How could she knowingly endanger his family? Look at what had just happened to Timothy O'Neill's friend.

But could she just pretend the explosion and this damned thing had nothing to do with Henson's murder? It had been *murder*. O'Neill had seen another man with Henson. One who'd been in control of the situation. Undoubtedly the same one who'd blown up his house.

Now or never. "Remember I told you there was something funny about that guy Crane's suicide scene? And that I'd given Henson a piece of evidence I thought might be relevant to his death."

"What was this evidence again? Something about the guy's eye?" Horns blared in the background. Patton muttered a curse.

Alex bit her lip. Did she tell him everything? Risk involving him despite what she knew could happen? So far everyone who'd touched this whatever the hell it was had either been murdered or nearly so.

Except her.

And that might very well only be because she'd just regained possession of the damned thing.

Okay. The decision was far too monumental to make in the next twenty or so seconds. Maybe she should sleep on it. She could talk to Patton after the memorial service tomorrow.

"It was…it was…" She scrambled to think of how to answer his question without telling him the truth. He'd clearly forgotten what she'd said earlier. "Just an eyeball." She winced at how lame that sounded.

"An eyeball?" The incredulity echoed in his voice.

"Yeah. I guess it turned out to be nothing."

She hoped he'd let it go at that. Obviously he hadn't really been listening to her when she'd visited him at the station, which might actually be a good thing. She needed to think about this some more.

"Wait a minute. You said he called you. That he was excited about this…eyeball. What gives, Alex? You're sure there isn't something you're not telling me?"

Shit. He'd called her Alex. None of the guys ever called her Alex unless they were suspicious or pissed.

Doing the right thing suddenly felt all wrong. She'd almost gone too far to back out. Somehow she had to take a major step back…at least for now.

"You know, Patton, I'd had a couple of beers last night. Maybe I misunderstood. I guess I was just so shocked to hear about his death that I got confused.

I should let you go. Give my best to your wife and daughter."

She hit the off button before he could argue.

She cursed herself for being so wishy-washy. She should have told him, but then he might have ended up dead, too.

"Stick with your plan, Alex," she muttered. She would sleep on it tonight and make a decision in the morning.

The memory of the pile of rubble that used to be O'Neill's home zoomed into vivid focus.

Maybe she and Marg should go to Shannon's house tonight.

What? And take the danger to her best friend?

Not a good idea.

At moments like this Alex really wished she owned a gun. She was usually antiweapons. You couldn't clean up cranial fragments and massive amounts of blood, which were usually the result of the use or misuse of firearms, and not be a little gun-shy.

She laid the phone back on the sink. First thing she had to do was hide the evidence.

If the guy who'd killed Henson showed up at her house he would likely know how to conduct a proper search. The idea that he might be from some government agency crossed her mind again, but she refused to blame this on the good guys until she knew more.

She needed a place most men wouldn't look.

Alex got down on her knees and dug around inside the sink cabinet until she found what she was looking for. A box of tampons.

Carefully, she pulled open one end and slid out the tampon. She removed the lower portion of the insertion tube, then gingerly slipped the contact lens from its plastic bag and tucked it into the larger section of the cardboard tube beneath the tampon. Using extreme caution she pushed the lower portion of the tube back into place and returned the whole thing into its plastic sleeve. She then tucked it, sealed end up, into the box, which she placed back under the sink.

She stood and, as she dusted her palms together, got a glimpse of herself in the mirror. She didn't like the uncertainty she saw there. For about two seconds she almost called Patton back and gave him the whole deal.

The doorbell chimed, saving her from having to decide.

"Saved by the bell," she muttered as she made her way to the living room.

She'd reached for the door when she considered that this could be trouble. Patton could have decided to stop by. Or it could be the guy who'd killed Henson. All right, she was getting paranoid here. Stay calm. Extra precautions were necessary, that was true, but there was no need to panic just yet.

In spite of her determination to stay calm her skin prickled with the trepidation that fizzed along her nerve endings.

Bracing herself, she leaned forward and peered through the peephole in her door.

The Professor.

Alex pulled the door open wide. "Hey." She kicked aside her murder theories and reminded herself to smile. "Is this a social call or is something wrong at work?"

His own smile was slow in coming. "A little of both perhaps."

She stepped back to clear him a path. "Come on in. I was just about to see what I could find in the fridge for dinner. You interested in joining me?" The abrupt yet overwhelming feeling came out of nowhere but she suddenly did not want to be alone this evening.

"I'm always interested in you, Alex." The Professor

entered her home and immediately took stock of the environment though he'd been there at least a dozen times before. "I do love this house," he noted aloud.

Alex believed him. He frequently commented on how fortunate she was to have such a lovely yet cozy home in this neighborhood. She wondered if he missed Boston or if he simply felt wistful for a place of his own. He lived in a three-story villa that, several decades ago, had been reinvented as apartments.

"Have a seat, Professor. Would you like a beer?"

Disapproval flashed briefly in his eyes. "As long as you serve it in a glass."

"Sure thing." Alex restrained her grin until she'd hustled off to the kitchen for refreshments. The Professor had grandiose ideas about how ladies and gentlemen should conduct themselves. Drinking beer from a bottle or, God forbid, a can did not quite reach the standards to which he clung.

That was just one of the things she liked about him.

He was intelligent, charming and had himself some definite standards. She had standards, as well. They just weren't as lofty as his.

As she poured the brew into a clean glass, stemmed no less, she wondered what prompted his move from

Boston. She'd considered asking him on occasion, but reminded herself that he told her from the beginning that he didn't like talking about his past.

At the time she'd hired him she had been desperate for help. Her business had just taken off and she couldn't afford to be choosy about personal lives. The man was meticulous at the job and that was all that had mattered at the time. Come to think of it, that was still pretty much all that mattered. The fact that she liked him, considered him part of the family actually, was just icing on the cake.

That was the thing Alex liked about Never Happened. The whole gang was like one big family. A shrink would probably say her employees filled a void since she'd grown up without any siblings or a father. Maybe that was a valid point. She definitely saw the Professor as father material.

Unfortunately her mother's taste had not run to the well-bred. She'd met Alex's father at a spring break binge. She'd sworn she was eighteen, and the college-freshman-turned-drop-out who'd become her father hadn't argued. The two had been bad for each other, plummeting into a hell-raising place of no return. Despite fifteen years of trying to survive together, her father had ultimately chosen to leave not only his little family, but the planet. Alex wasn't sure she would ever forgive him for that. Just another reason not to count on anything or anyone. If a girl couldn't count on her own father, who could she count on?

Yes, her father had been far different from the man keeping her company just now. While the Professor had been achieving the distinguished career letters that no doubt accompanied his official signature, her father had been drinking, drugging and chasing college girls on spring break. Alex wasn't sure she could have tolerated him as long as Marg had. But her mother's tolerance of her father's no-good ways had come at a price.

One both she and Alex were still paying.

Shrugging off the past, Alex returned to the living room, glasses brimming. "Here ya go." She presented her guest with his drink, then settled into a chair across from the sofa where he'd made himself comfortable. He wore his usual khaki trousers, crisply starched white shirt and navy bow tie. The only variation in his wardrobe was the Argyle sweater he wore in the winter.

While they drank in silence, Alex couldn't keep her mind off the piece of evidence she'd hidden beneath her bathroom sink. What did it mean? Who wanted it back? Surely no one in the United States government had killed to get it back. That kind of scenario only happened in the movies.

Timothy's words echoed in her head, challenging her conclusion.

"What's the story with Detective Henson?"

That the Professor asked that question startled her when it probably shouldn't have. "He had an accident." There she went going all lame again. The Professor knew he'd had an accident. He was the one to tell her, but she couldn't answer his questions just now.

He studied her, his gaze more probing than she would have liked. "Is what happened to Henson why you've been so distracted today?"

Alex sipped her beer, buying some time. The Professor read them all a little too well, but he generally kept his comments to himself. Was she so transparent that he could so easily see the emotional turmoil this situation had caused? She'd thought her actions today had been normal. She'd done her job, hadn't made any mistakes that she was aware of.

She drew her brow into a thoughtful frown. "Did I seem distracted?"

This was her chance. She could share her troubling secret with someone, get a feel for the believability of the whole thing…but she couldn't.

She couldn't endanger anyone else's life until she had considered exactly what her next step should be.

Maybe she should go straight to the FBI, just skip the locals altogether.

"The owner of the apartment building in Carol City called just before five. He needed to know if you were coming by his office to collect payment since he was about to leave for the day."

The revelation spun over her like a steamroller. She'd forgotten to collect the payment for the remains she'd cleaned up this afternoon. In all the years she'd been in business she'd never once forgotten to collect.

The Professor must have read the astonishment on her face since he added, "Don't worry, Shannon was ready to leave for the day so she dropped by to take care of the collection."

Alex winced inwardly. That meant Shannon knew she'd been off her game, as well. It was a miracle her phone hadn't rung already.

As if reading her mind he said, "Shannon and her husband have that neighborhood watch meeting tonight."

Alex checked the clock. The meeting would be over by eight. Her phone would be ringing by eight-ten.

The silence thickened between them. She could feel the weight of the Professor's question bearing down on her. Both he and Shannon would know she'd been seriously distracted. She should just fess up and get it over with. The whole thing was bound to come out eventually.

Assuming she lived long enough to see it through.

A chill washed over her. Was her life really in danger? The excitement she'd heard in Henson's voice last night nudged at her. All that Timothy O'Neill had said strong-armed into her worrisome thoughts, too.

"Something strange happened last night." That was a whopping understatement. "It started with that suicide cleanup. You know, Charlie Crane?"

The Professor nodded. His scarcely touched beer sat on the coffee table now. She had to start keeping some wine around the house for unexpected visitors who preferred something more refined than her favorite beer.

"I found his left eyeball at the scene." Now for the sci-fi bit. "There was an odd sort of…" She shifted.

"It looked like a contact lens only larger and thicker. Kind of metallic-looking around the perimeter."

He crossed one leg over the other, showing a length of white sock along with a well-polished brown leather loafer. "I assume you gave this unusual item to the detective in charge of the case."

Her head was moving up and down before he finished his statement. "Rich Henson."

The Professor stroked his clean-shaven chin. His sandy-colored hair was more gray now than anything, but it was full and well kept. "This is why he called you last night?"

She remembered saying that she'd just spoken to him the night before when she read the article in the *Herald* about his death. "He called to thank me. He thought it might actually be a computer chip or something. He'd taken it to a friend in Morningside who did the occasional unofficial analysis for him."

"I see." He clasped his hands together on his knee. "This is why you were interested in the explosion over in Morningside."

Did her crew all sit around and discuss what Alex was up to whenever she was out of the office or was this just one of those days when no one had anything better to do?

"Yeah. I went over there. Talked to a few of the neighbors. The guy, Timothy O'Neill, was a computer geek who apparently worked out of his basement."

"Henson is killed in a freak one-car accident and his friend's house blows up." The Professor studied her a moment. "You think it somehow has something to do with the lens."

This was as far as she intended to go. He didn't need to know that Timothy was still alive or that the chip-lens was hidden in her bathroom. "I'm certain of it. It's too coincidental otherwise." She heaved a woebegone sigh. "His partner thinks he just fell asleep at the wheel. But the accident occurred only a little while after he called me. He was wide-awake and hyped when I talked to him. There's no way he fell asleep at the wheel."

"You've told this to his partner?"

Back to sticky territory. How much should she tell him? "Most of it," she admitted.

He twiddled his thumbs as he mulled over what she'd said so far. She hoped he wouldn't ask any more questions. She really hated to lie to the Professor.

"The way I see it," he offered, "the only option you have is telling Henson's partner the whole story and leaving it in his hands. Without Henson or this

Timothy fellow or the evidence, there's very little you can do, Alex."

Even with the evidence she felt as if her hands were tied. "I know. I feel totally helpless."

The Professor stood. "Well, if there's anything I can do please let me know." His gaze held hers a moment before he turned toward the door. "It's not easy losing a friend so abruptly."

As she watched the Professor drive away she wondered if he had lost a friend. He'd sounded exactly as if he'd lost someone close and could fully imagine how she felt. She was the only one in denial.

Just another unanswered question in the secret life of her esteemed Professor.

Strange, she decided, how you never really knew a person. Not even yourself.

Except for the dead, of course. Nothing was sacred once a person had stopped breathing. Officials or relatives, sometimes both, pilfered through their belongings. M.E.s and their technicians picked through their remains.

She looked around her living room. What would her home, her belongings reveal about her?

That she lived pretty damned well in a town where money was everything. That she was, at times, vain to a fault. That she lived alone and liked it…most of the time. That as tough as she wanted to look to survive in this man's ego-driven world her work hauled her smack into the middle of, she wasn't always.

Everyone had secrets and fears they didn't want anyone else to know about.

She had her share. Not being as vulnerable as her mother had been was one. Financial security was another. She wanted to stand on her own two feet and never allow anyone or anything to hold her back.

So, yeah, she had secrets. Good and bad.

She thought of the lens she'd hidden in her bathroom. But not all secrets would get you killed.

Enough with the self-analyzing already. She had to get her mind on something else.

Marg was home. She should check in on her. Her unexplained absences today could mean trouble.

Alex locked the door behind her as she left, something she never did when her destination was just up a flight of stairs to Marg's apartment. But the idea that whoever had killed Henson might be watching her was enough to have her taking a few precautions.

She hustled up the steps to Marg's door and

knocked. The evening news blared from the television so she knocked again just in case the first one hadn't been loud enough.

The door opened and Marg looked startled as if she hadn't expected anyone to be at the door. "Alex?"

The purse hanging from her mother's shoulder and the keys dangling from her hand told Alex that her mother was going out for the evening. None of that surprised her; what did, however, was the state of her dress. Sweatpants and a T-shirt. Marg never wore sweatpants or a tee unless she was going to the gym. And she hadn't gone to the gym in ages.

"Were you on your way out?" Seemed like a good starting place.

Marg blinked. "Yes. Yes I am."

Well there was an informative answer. "Plans with Robert?" Impossible. The sweatpants alone negated that possibility, but maybe the question would prompt an answer.

"No." Marg scooted out the door, forcing Alex to step aside. She locked the door and turned to her daughter. "You know, Alex, I never ask you about the men you date. I certainly don't attempt to keep tabs on your comings and goings. I believe I deserve the same respect for my privacy."

Alex opened her mouth to give her a load of reasons why it wasn't the same thing, but her mother held up a hand to silence her.

"I know I've made a lot of mistakes," Marg went on, "but I'm on my feet now. I can take care of myself. I don't need a babysitter."

Alex took a breath. Decided not to start an argument. "I worry, so shoot me."

Marg hitched the strap of her purse a little higher on her shoulder. "We're not that different, you know. You just don't want to see it. If you look really close you'll see just how much alike we are."

Alex watched her mother descend the stairs and cross the street to where she'd left her car at the curb, then she drove away.

Today had been strange and unnerving in a lot of ways, but outside of Henson's death nothing about it had rattled her as badly as this.

If you look really close you'll see just how much alike we are.

They were aeons apart. Why couldn't Marg see that?

Alex stamped back down to her own front door.

She had been working hard for her entire adult life to show just how different she and her mother were. Marg would never even consider facing danger to prove a friend had been murdered. She'd run like hell.

Alex wasn't running. She would find out the truth.

CHAPTER 7

St. Mary's Cathedral over on Second Avenue was not only a place of worship it was a beautiful church. Alex had been here only one other time but she hadn't forgotten the lovely faceted glass or the panels of metal, mosaic and ivory embellishing the chapel altar. Handcrafted gold and precious stone illustrations of the life of Christ as well as glass mosaics depicting scenes from Mary's life adorned the tabernacle.

She wasn't sure Henson would have appreciated the illustrious setting or the somber atmosphere, but he would have gotten a hell of a kick out of all the attention.

The place was packed in every available chamber. All of Miami's finest, dressed in their classiest garb, had come out to pay their final respects. The flames dancing atop the lit candles flickered from the gold candlesticks, glinting off the crucifix holding court behind the priest who offered consoling words for the friends and family of the fallen detective.

She spotted Jimmy Patton near the front as she surveyed the hundreds upon hundreds in attendance.

Could one of the men standing in this very church be the one who'd accompanied Henson to Timothy O'Neill's home? Would he be watching her and wondering what she knew or didn't know?

Since there had been no report in this morning's headlines of Timothy having turned himself in, she could only assume that he'd followed through on his vow that he intended to disappear. Not that she could blame him. Someone had tried to kill him, had killed his friend.

She'd thought this whole situation over last night, ensuring that she'd slept very little. Her decision was that she would give the whole story to Patton but she would keep the evidence tucked safely in her bathroom for now. She just couldn't risk letting it out of her possession. It was the only proof she had of her suspicions. All she really wanted was for Patton to take a closer look at the cause of Henson's accident. If he believed the accident was no accident, then that would ensure a full investigation.

Until she saw further, that was all she was prepared to do. If he refused to believe her, well then she'd have to regroup and try another tactic. She might very well end up having to give him the lens, but that would be a last resort for now. She had to protect her interests while protecting anyone else whose life the lens might endanger. Henson was dead. As much as she wanted the man responsible for his death to pay, endangering anyone else at this point didn't feel like the right thing to do. Henson would agree with her. She had to do this for him. The key element in her investigation was ensuring that she didn't do anything rash. The lens alone didn't prove anything. The so-called accident and explosion were the two elements the police needed to focus on. If she could somehow make Patton see the connection, that would be a tremendous step in the right direction.

The other big question left up in the air was, did the mystery man who'd killed Henson and Timothy's other friend know about her involvement?

Had Henson told him where he'd gotten the lens?

Probably not, she decided, since no one had approached her. Henson had likely protected her. She had to see this through for him. She owed it to him. He'd been a great guy and hadn't deserved to go that way.

She wished now that she had questioned Timothy O'Neill a bit more. Since Henson hadn't taken the lens to the police lab and he hadn't spoken to his partner about it, she had to assume that the analysis O'Neill had done had tipped off the bad guy. O'Neill had either called someone and asked questions or looked for information on the Internet. Whichever strategy he'd used, a red flag had gone up and brought the enemy to his door.

But the enemy had brought Henson along for the ride. So was it something Henson did or said that prompted the bad guy or was it O'Neill?

There wasn't any way to know the answer to that question. She doubted she could find O'Neill again if she tried. The cops thought he was dead. That was another thing she couldn't do. She couldn't rat out O'Neill. As long as the bad guy or guys thought he was dead the kid was safe. He'd already lost his best friend. He deserved a break.

What she could tell Patton was looking less and less substantial.

As the service came to a close a man hurried up the aisle to where Detective Patton now stood. Alex didn't recognize the guy until he turned slightly to speak with Patton.

Detective Winston from the scene where the explosion had taken place. Mr. Smart-ass.

He said something for Patton's ears only and the two rushed out of the sanctuary. The main aisle filled behind them as if the two men had somehow given the crowd gathered an order of dismissal with their hasty exit.

Alex didn't bother fighting the crowd to catch up. She could touch base with Patton at his office. Besides, the discussion they needed to have would be best in private. Then again, Winston could have arrived with news related to the case. Since he had been working the scene of the explosion, maybe he had learned that the victim pulled from the ashes was not Timothy O'Neill.

If that were the case, technically she could tell Patton what O'Neill had said without outing him.

Eventually the final row in front of her emptied and her opportunity to file into the exit line presented itself.

Outside, the sun blazed like Hades itself. Black wasn't exactly a great color in the heat of a Miami summer day. But then, no well-groomed lady went to a funeral or memorial service wearing anything else. Black dress, scoop neck, capped sleeves and midthigh in length. And what savvy fashionista would be caught dead in a little black dress without the matching stilettos? Alex had chosen her favorite pair, a black-and-white zebra pattern on the outside, contrasted by blood-red lining inside. Classy and undeniably sexy. Henson would have approved. That too-familiar pang of regret tugged at her.

Miami's esteemed mayor as well as every high-ranking member of Miami-Dade brass mingled in the parking area. She'd heard various and sundry comments about what a shame the accident had been, and asides as to how much Rich Henson would be missed.

Alex shook her head. All those cops and not one had a clue that Henson had been murdered.

It seemed impossible. Whoever had done this knew how to fool everyone.

Patton's hasty dash out of the church slid to the front of her thoughts. Maybe at least one of Henson's colleagues sensed that something wasn't quite right.

Not necessarily, though, she argued. Winston was working the O'Neill explosion. Patton, the Henson accident. To her knowledge, the two investigations hadn't been connected. Maybe they'd found something new that would connect the two. Either way, she wouldn't get to talk to Patton now.

"Well, damn," she muttered. She almost bit her tongue when she considered that she was scarcely out the door of God's house and here she was swearing.

She glanced skyward and mumbled a *sorry*. Not that He wouldn't expect her to swear. She'd learned how to cut a guy off at the knees with nothing more than her razor-sharp tongue long ago. Despite her career, she considered herself antiviolence. Maybe that would count for something even though about the only time she came to church was when someone died. Except for the christening of Shannon's children. Thank God Shannon and her husband hadn't died on her. As the kids' godmother, Alex would have been next in line for bringing them up.

She wasn't really into the mother thing. She still didn't understand why Shannon had picked her.

"One of the great mysteries of the universe," she mumbled as she strolled across the lot to her 4Runner.

"Damned hot day for wearing black."

Alex's head came up and her gaze collided with a stranger leaning against a red Mercedes SL500 parked next to her 4Runner. As she watched, he reached up and removed a pair of aviator sunglasses.

The black suit he wore was expensively cut. She

didn't have to touch it to recognize the fabric as silk. A designer label carrying a hefty price tag no doubt. A narrow black tie contrasted a white shirt that looked crisp and fresh in spite of the sweltering humidity. About the only clue the guy wasn't blessed with his own personal bubble of refrigerated air was the fine beads of sweat gathered on his forehead.

And what a nice forehead he had. Broad, but not too much so. Square jaw, long, straight nose. Nice lips, though she doubted they smiled often. His expression was too…something. Not exactly hard or rigid…controlled. Yes. That was the word for this stranger. Controlled.

Even the wide-set blue eyes were masked in a cordial look of politeness. The beach-bum blond hair was military short, kind of spiky.

The image of her running her fingers through that thick spiky hair while making this guy lose control abruptly flashed in her naughty mind.

Jesus. First she was swearing not twenty feet from the church doors, now she was having sexual fantasies halfway across the parking lot.

She was definitely going to hell.

"Can't wear anything else to a memorial service." She walked past him, feeling the weight and heat of his stare, and paused at the driver's side door of her 4Runner.

"You have a flat."

Startled that he'd followed her around to the other side of her vehicle, she jumped a little. That ticked her off. More so that he recognized he'd surprised her than the fact that he had.

His words penetrated her irritation and she stared down at her rear tire. Flat. The rim sat all the way down on the asphalt.

How the hell had that happened? And why hadn't she noticed? Because she'd been too busy checking out the handsome stranger.

All four tires had been fine when she'd arrived just over an hour ago.

"That's why I was hanging around." He strolled closer, his hands in his pockets. "I thought whoever owned this SUV might need some assistance."

"I have AAA." She reached into her red leather shoulder bag and fished out her phone. "Thanks anyway," she said to him. "I wouldn't want you to soil your nice suit."

"I don't mind at all. Triple-A could take hours to get here."

That much was true. She'd once sat on the

causeway for ninety minutes waiting for the serviceman to arrive. Then again, the serviceman had been
a great date that same night.

Not about to let the guy think he could do something she couldn't, she clarified the situation. "I
could change it myself if not for the dress." No point
in giving the good folks lingering around St. Mary's
a show to watch.

"I'm sure you could handle most anything that
came your way, Miss…?" He inclined his head and
studied her as he waited for her response.

"Alex." She shifted her cellular phone to her left
hand and stuck out her right. "Alex Jackson."

He gripped her hand. Nice. Smooth skin, firm
grip. "Austin Blake."

With her stiletto advantage she stood practically
eye to eye with him. She guessed his height at five-
ten or eleven. Maybe a hundred eighty pounds.
Athletic. She based that last assessment more on the
way he moved than anything else since the jacket
concealed about everything but the breadth of his
shoulders.

She dropped her phone back into her bag. "I guess
I'll take you up on your offer if you're sure you don't
mind."

The jacket came off and she got a tantalizing visual confirmation as to his lean athleticism. The white shirt fitted his torso as if it had been tailor-made just for him.

"It would be my pleasure." He passed his jacket to her and strode toward the rear cargo door.

Curiosity propelling her she checked out the label. Versace. Good grief. Who was this guy?

Her movements impeded by her thoughts, she moved slowly toward the rear of her vehicle. He'd already removed the spare and the necessary tools for the job to come and placed them on the asphalt.

"Excuse me." He moved around her to crouch down by the damaged tire.

"Tell me, Mr. Blake—" she propped against the side of her SUV "—what does a guy who wears Versace and drives a car that cost six figures do? Can't be a cop."

She was being nosy, but what the heck? A girl could never be wary enough of strangers offering gifts or assistance. Even if the offered assistance was on holy ground.

With the SUV jacked up, he'd already started to loosen the lug nuts when he glanced up at her. "You think a cop can't be independently wealthy?"

Okay, he had her there. Miami was the home of the rich and infamous. He could be the bad boy son of some mogul. The thing was she kept an eye on the social pages and she'd never heard of him.

It was her one weakness when it came to current events—she adored gossip. Whether international celebrities or local heiresses, she couldn't get enough of reading about them. No one—absolutely no one—knew that little secret. Shannon, who read nothing but nonfiction, would never let her live it down. It was an easy addiction to conceal since Marg bought every gossip rag on the newsstand. Marg too often borrowed Alex's clothes, but Alex borrowed her magazines and papers. The difference was Marg never knew.

Alex had to work with Shannon and the Professor every day…no way was she letting them learn that tidbit to tease her about. And tease they would.

"So you're a cop." She straightened away from the vehicle and planted one stiletto-clad foot slightly in front of her. The move accomplished her goal, his gaze traced a path from her ankle to the hem of her dress. "With Miami-Dade County? Miami Beach? North Beach?"

He loosened the last nut with a firm twist of the

lug wrench. "Let's just say my jurisdiction supersedes local law enforcement."

Oh, ho. The man was a fed. She should have gotten that one. Most feds were classy dressers. Then again, Versace went a little above and beyond mere classy.

"FBI?"

She had to admit she was rather enjoying this little game of twenty questions. Took her mind off the depressing current events in her life.

"You know I'm in law enforcement." He pulled the flat tire free and set it aside. "Why don't you tell me what you do for a living?"

She laughed. "Maybe because I'm not sure you'll believe me." No one ever guessed her occupation.

He slid the spare tire into place before meeting her gaze. "You're a professional cleaner."

The wariness she'd let slide bumped back up a notch. "What makes you say that?"

"I smelled a hint of something stronger than the garden-variety disinfectant when I opened your cargo door."

As hard as she tried she couldn't keep her vehicle completely free of the hazards of her work. That was why she'd had a special partition installed between the backseat and the cargo area. At least she could keep any lingering odors out of the passenger compartment.

"You guessed it, I'm a cleaner." For all he knew she was a maid. Half the Hispanic population made good wages keeping the homes of the Miami elite spit-and-polished.

"But not just any kind of cleaner," he went on as he gave the lug wrench a violent twist to tighten a third nut back into place.

"My turn," she countered. "You knew Detective Henson?"

"Are we still playing the guessing game or am I supposed to give you a straight answer?"

The more he relaxed the more charm he allowed into his eyes. His smile almost looked genuine now. Some of that fierce control had melted. Maybe from the heat rising from the asphalt.

"A straight answer would be nice."

"I'm investigating his death."

No way could she have reacted quickly enough to veil her expression. "What do you mean? He had an accident, right? That's what the papers said."

"Did he?" He locked another nut into place with enough pressure to match an air wrench.

"His partner seems to think so." She was hedging.

Whatever this guy knew, he was on a digging expedition. Her gaze narrowed. His parking and then waiting by her vehicle was no coincidence, she deduced, any more than the flat tire had been.

"But you don't think so." He tightened the final lug nut and popped the wheel cover into place.

Her wariness had shot to full scale alert now. Who was this guy?

Shrugging casually, she refused to confirm what could only be his theory. "I don't agree with the idea that he fell asleep at the wheel," she admitted. The only way this fed could know anything was if Patton had told him what she'd said about talking to Henson the night of the accident. "Henson and I spoke briefly and he sounded fine. It's my understanding the accident occurred a short time later. He just didn't sound sleepy or even tired to me."

Blake stood, grabbed the flat tire and walked around her to heft it into the cargo area. He picked up the tools next and put them away before saying more.

He swiped his palms together to dust them off. "What did you talk about?"

Uncertain as to just how much she should share with this handsome stranger, she hesitated a couple seconds too long.

"I could obtain a warrant."

A warrant? "You're going to arrest me to get the details of a personal telephone conversation?" Why were the feds suddenly interested in Henson's accident?

Government stuff. The kind of stuff we civilians aren't supposed to see if we want to stay alive.

Maybe Timothy O'Neill was more right than he knew.

"I wouldn't have to arrest you, Alex," Blake said as he closed the cargo door. "I could bring you in as a person of interest to the case."

"To what case?" She tossed the words back at him, still refusing to admit to anything more than what she'd said already. "Why didn't Detective Patton say anything about Henson's accident being under further investigation?"

There was something wrong about this whole situation. Anger started to simmer low in her gut. If Patton had suspected something he should have told her. He had no business leaving her in the dark like this.

Then again, she had pretty much left him in the dark.

"Detective Patton only knows what he needs to know. This is my investigation. The locals have been instructed as to the hands-off nature," Blake said, drawing her away from her frustrating thoughts. He reached for his jacket and folded it neatly over his left arm.

The mixture of irritation and wariness had just given way to something a little more significant— like outrage—when another idea kicked its way into her evolving conclusions.

This could be *the man*.

The man who'd arrived at the O'Neill home with Henson. The same one who'd killed him.

"Thanks for taking care of the tire." She stretched her lips into a fake smile. "I'd love to stay and chat some more, but I have an appointment."

Call her dramatic, but she had to say that when Blake reached into the interior pocket of his jacket— even though she'd held said jacket and knew he couldn't possibly have been carrying a weapon without her noticing the additional weight—her breath caught.

"Take my card." He held out an elegantly embossed business card. "I'd like you to call me if you remember anything that might be helpful to this case."

She reached for the card, but he held on to it long enough to add, "I'm quite certain you want to see justice done."

He released the card and walked away.

Alex was still standing there when he drove off in his sporty red Mercedes.

She stared down at the card. It told her two things. His name and a telephone number, mobile probably.

Shouldn't Federal Bureau of Investigations be inscribed on the card?

If only O'Neill had gotten a look at the guy who'd been with Henson. She couldn't be sure if this Blake character was a good guy or a bad guy.

What she needed now was to talk to Patton. If the feds were investigating Henson's accident, the locals would have to know. Blake had said as much, called his investigation hands-off as far as the locals were concerned.

Alex slid behind the wheel of her 4Runner and cranked the engine. She set the air-conditioning to maximum and dug for her phone. With Miami Beach PD on speed dial, she entered the necessary number and pushed her hair behind her shoulders to let the cooling air flow over her throat.

When Patton came on the line, she didn't mince words. "Hey, why didn't you tell me that the feds were investigating Henson's accident?"

A heavy sigh echoed across the line. "What the hell are you talking about, Alex?"

Alex. She saw how it was.

"I'm talking about this guy Blake. He grilled me in the church parking lot. You could have told me last night when I called."

"Look." Another deep breath. "I haven't the slightest idea what you're talking about. We're all upset that Henson is dead. I know the memorial service was tough on everyone. But for Christ's sake, Alex, you've got to stop making things worse by coming up with these accusations. Henson is dead. So far it just looks like a tragic accident."

"You didn't sic some fed on me about that call Henson made to me the night he died?"

"Of course not. Why would the feds be involved in this case anyway?" Patton sounded tired. Tired and disgusted. "Like I told you before, we're checking out every aspect of the accident. If anything—and I mean anything—was out of sync we'll find it."

But they wouldn't find it. Not only were they looking in the wrong place, they had no idea what they were looking for.

CHAPTER 8

One of the nicest things about being unattached was the fact that you didn't have to let anybody know when you were coming or when you were going. You just did what you wanted to do.

Alex parked in her driveway and strode up the walk to her front door. She didn't have to answer to anyone but herself. It was the most liberating feeling in the world. She liked having that power over her destiny.

She'd worked hard to gain her financial freedom. The road hadn't always been easy, but that made victory all the sweeter.

As she unlocked her front door she wondered how any woman could tolerate the compromises of monogamous commitment. Alex just didn't get it. Men were great. She loved men! But there were far too many out there to simply settle for one.

Maybe that was a selfish attitude but there was no

point in lying to herself. She knew what she liked and she went after it.

Take Blake for example. A guy like him could be a challenge. Intriguing on a number of levels. The whole mystery behind who he was and what he actually did for a living could jump-start the most lethargic libido. She could just imagine how many layers of control concealed the real man beneath that expensive suit.

He was the kind of guy a girl would have to get to one layer at a time.

The possibility that he could be Henson's killer had her chucking all thoughts of how sexy the guy was. As interesting as he was, the only thing she really wanted to know about Blake right now was whether or not he'd had anything to do with Henson's murder. At this point she was reasonably sure that launching a murder investigation of her own was the only way one would happen. Patton was not picking up on her hints. Whatever was going on, somehow Patton was completely out of the loop.

Considering everyone in the loop but her and the killer were either dead or presumed dead, Patton's position was more than a little advantageous.

She, Alex considered as she closed and locked

the door behind her, was in a far more precarious situation. If Blake suspected she knew something, who else did? The man who had killed Henson. Probably the same one who'd blown up the O'Neill home.

This, of course, was assuming Blake wasn't the bad guy. She knew herself well enough to know that her readiness to give him the benefit of the doubt had way too much to do with his charisma.

Not a good thing under the circumstances.

Her mother's comment about how alike they were nagged at her but she ignored it. They were total opposites. Anyone who knew them would say the same. Alex liked being in control. She liked standing on her own two feet. She liked doing things her way.

Her mother was rarely in control of her destiny. She was wholly dependent upon Alex for a place to live and a job. Her relationships always ended badly.

'Nuff said.

Alex tossed her bag onto the sofa and kicked off her stilettos. She'd peel off the dress later. First she wanted a beer and something to crunch on. She'd totally forgotten lunch except for a bag of chips, and grease didn't, technically, count as a food group.

She grabbed a Michelob from the fridge and quenched her thirst. After throwing together a ham sandwich and snagging her shoes she headed to her room to get comfortable with the stack of magazines she'd borrowed from Marg's apartment. She smiled. Even if she died tonight, Shannon would just assume Marg had left the gossip rags at Alex's house or that Alex had confiscated them for some reason.

She stopped. Just because both she and Marg liked the gossip rags didn't mean they were alike.

They were nothing alike.

Not that Alex felt hostile toward her mother, not at all. She simply recognized the glaring differences, like Marg's total dependence on others while Alex was überindependent.

She wasn't going to think about that anymore. She went into her room and put the shoes away in her closet, set her half-empty beer and sandwich aside and was just about to wiggle out of her dress when she noticed the earring glittering on the carpet.

It was one of those freak things. The tiny gold-and-pearl stud was so small it was a miracle she saw it at all. Somehow her gaze just happened to land in the right spot and recognition fired in the only two brain cells she had left that were paying attention.

She bent down and picked it up. Since she remembered well that she hadn't worn those particular earrings in ages, months even, her face gathered into a frown.

Placing the earring on the top of her jewelry box, she opened the first dresser drawer—the one where she kept her panties. Things appeared in order. She recalled that two nights ago she'd noticed that her mother had messed with her stuff. She'd meant to mention that to her and she'd forgotten.

Determined to be sure her mother hadn't borrowed anything else, Alex went through drawer after drawer. The more she opened and slammed closed, the angrier she got. It wasn't so much a particular garment or item out of place it was the keen awareness that her things had been moved…touched.

She marched to her closet next. Oh, Marg had been careful. Every dress, blouse, pair of slacks and shoes was exactly where they were supposed to be, but Alex could sense the change, however subtle. A triumphant smile slid across her lips when her gaze lit on the pink suit Marg had borrowed for her third date with Robert.

Alex checked her jewelry box. Not that she had anything expensive, but just to see if Marg had actually borrowed a pair of earrings or if she'd just been looking to see if Alex had bought anything new lately.

The frown laid claim to her face again. Now this was where her mother had fallen down on covering her tracks. The earrings were paired together but not in the same place they'd been. Not that Alex was a neat freak or anything but she kept the ones she wore most often on top, the rest in the bottom compartment.

She slammed the box shut, finished off her sandwich and beer to give herself a couple minutes to cool off, then she stormed out the front door and straight up to Marg's apartment. A couple of bangs later and her mother came to the door, wearing a jade sheath that fit like a second skin and a pair of Alex's shoes she'd completely forgotten about since they'd been gone from her closet for so long.

"I wondered where those had gotten to," she said, giving the green snakeskin shoes a confirming glance.

"Alex! I borrowed them from you for the Christmas party. Don't you remember?"

Marg Jackson looked fantastic in the outfit. Her figure was remarkable for a woman her age, with or without a gym membership. Even her face lacked the usual wrinkles associated with AARP eligibility and years in the Florida sun. She had to hand it to her mother, the woman swore by SPF 45 or above sunblock. No matter how great the genes, sun damage could ruin the prettiest face.

"That was Christmas before last," Alex reminded. "And you haven't returned them yet."

"I promise I'll have them back to you tomorrow. Right now I have to go. I'm meeting some friends for dinner."

Suspicion overrode the bone Alex had to pick with her mother. "What friends?" She hadn't heard Marg talking about any new friends. And all her old friends were party girls who lived to drink and vice versa.

"New friends," she returned. "You don't know them."

"I don't have dinner plans," Alex suggested. "Maybe I could meet your friends, as well."

Marg looked nervous. Dammit. Alex wanted to shake her. When would she learn? She couldn't keep screwing up. There had to come a time when she realized that she was wasting her life on booze and bad relationships. As far as Alex was concerned that time was now.

"Okay," Marg admitted, "you've outted me. These aren't new friends. It's a support group."

"AA?" Alex was shocked. Her mother had outright refused to join Alcoholics Anonymous. She'd insisted the group was for those too weak to quit drinking on their own. What had changed her mind? Or maybe this was a trick. "Which group?"

Marg exhaled an impatient breath and dug a card from her purse. Alex shook her head as she realized the purse was hers, too. Of course her mother would borrow it, it matched the shoes.

"Here." She shoved the card at Alex.

SDA. What the hell? Sexual Dysfunction Association. About five more seconds were required before she fully absorbed what she'd just read. She shifted her attention back to her mother, who looked less than pleased to have been discovered.

"This is good." It was all Alex could think to say. Apparently Richard Simmons hadn't been enough.

Marg snatched the card back. "We'll see. You know I don't put much stock in support groups."

That she was even going was a flat-out miracle. "I'm glad you're making the effort."

Marg gave a little smirk. "Maybe you should join, too." She stepped out onto the stoop.

Incensed, Alex huffed. "There's absolutely nothing wrong with my sex life."

"Really?" Marg gave her a haughty look. "I suppose you consider avoiding commitment at your age normal?"

"Yes." Yes, she did. Just because she was forty didn't mean she had to be married. There were no rules this day and time about how old was too old to still be single.

Marg made a dismissive sound as she locked her door behind her. "Denial is a powerful enemy."

Her mother stepped around her and started down the stairs. Alex stared after her in astonishment for two beats before understanding bobbed to the surface. Marg had done that to change the subject.

"Hey!" Alex marched down the steps after her. "We're not finished yet."

At the bottom of the steps, Marg turned to face her daughter. "Make it fast I don't want to be late."

"Look." Alex forced herself to be calm. This was her mother. No need to get nasty, even if she had played the commitment card. "You know I don't mind when you borrow my clothes and stuff."

"I always get whatever I borrow cleaned," Marg cut in. "And I never lose or damage anything."

Alex thought about the earring but decided to let that go. She'd dropped her share in the past. "True.

But I don't like you coming into my house and going through my stuff without asking first."

Marg threw up her hands. "I went straight to your closet and got the pink suit then returned it the very next day. I didn't touch anything else."

And just moments ago she'd been taking Alex down the road about denial. "Mother—"

Marg cleared her throat in warning.

"Marg, you jumbled up my jewelry box. You went through my drawers. Just admit it and we'll get past it. I can let it slide this time."

Okay, Alex realized that she was being hypocritical considering she'd borrowed—and she used the term in its loosest form—her mother's magazines without asking. But that was different. She went behind her back to protect her secret. Marg just did it because she was Marg, she thought the world revolved around her.

"I did not touch your jewelry box." She folded her arms over her ample chest. "I did not open a single one of your drawers. I went straight to your closet and took the pink suit. I had my own pink sandals. And I borrowed these shoes ages ago."

Alex started to argue with her, but the fury in her mother's eyes stopped her. Marg was telling the truth.

About the only thing she'd ever lied to Alex about anyway was her drinking.

"So you haven't been in my stuff."

Marg shook her head adamantly from side to side.

Something far too close to fear flashed through Alex. "I apologize for accusing you. I just thought…"

Concern marred her mother's smooth complexion. "You think someone has gone through your things?"

Alex shrugged and laughed it off. There was no need to upset Marg. She was taking a big step going to this support group. The last thing Alex wanted to do was give her an excuse not to go.

"I'm probably overreacting."

Marg patted her arm. "We've all noticed how upset you've been about the death of your detective friend. You should just relax this weekend. Rescue Shannon from domestic slavery and go to a spa."

Well there was an idea. "Maybe I will."

When Marg would have headed toward her sexy Miata, Alex grabbed her and hugged her. "I want you to know I'm really proud of you for taking this step."

Her mother drew back, looking a little startled and a lot suspect. "Are you sure you're okay, Alex?"

Alex laughed again, the sound strained. "I'm fine.

Go. I'll do like you said and drag Shannon away from the house for the evening."

"Good."

Alex watched her mother drive away in her sporty red car. Blake's Mercedes had been that same shade of sexy red.

Was he the one who'd gone through her house?

Okay, maybe she was letting her imagination run away with her. She needed a heavy dose of reality.

Who better to give it to her than Shannon?

Shannon Bainbridge and her husband, Bobby, lived in a Mediterranean style house in north Miami Beach. Quiet neighborhood, good schools and escalating real estate values.

Shannon's kids, a boy and a girl, were off in college, one at Florida State the other at Georgia Tech, both on academic scholarships. Husband Bobby worked in construction and had achieved the status of project manager. Until Alex opened Never Happened Shannon had been a domestic engineer.

Since the kids had already been in high school, Alex concluded that she had saved her friend from a life of boring sameness—cleaning, cooking and shopping.

Alex rang the bell and took the time to appreciate Shannon's gorgeous landscaping. The woman had it going on outside and in. It was part of her Type A personality. Everything had to be perfect.

Every vine, every flowering shrub and potted plant served a curb-appeal purpose. The same space-conscious attitude defined the interior. From the architectural features of the ceilings and the paint on the walls to the gleaming tile on the floor, not a single opportunity to impress had been missed.

Bobby had the know-how but Shannon had the vision.

The red paneled door swung open wide. "Alex! What're you doing here?"

"You're not on your way out, are you?" Alex knew the answer before she asked. Shannon and Bobby went out one night per week and tonight wasn't it. They had a schedule for everything, even sex. The scary thing was they never deviated. Is that what happened after twenty-odd years of marriage?

"Absolutely not. Come in." She ushered Alex inside and closed the door. "Bobby!"

Her obedient husband sauntered into the entry hall. "Alex! You're looking mighty fine."

She'd changed before heading this way. Jeans,

tank and thonged sandals. Thank God Shannon didn't mind her husband's gawking. That was another thing that appeared to evolve the longer a couple was together—the length of time a man's gaze was allowed to stray.

Shannon elbowed him to get his attention. "Put another steak on the grill."

Bobby glanced at his wife. "Okay. Sure."

Shannon grabbed Alex by the hand. "Come on, we'll have a glass of wine."

Her friend's kitchen was large and homey. Lots of travertine and slate, lots of spacious honey-colored cabinets. A working kitchen. Shannon was a self-taught chef. Her husband's round form testified to that fact.

Alex climbed onto a stool at the kitchen island. Shannon settled two stemmed glasses on the granite surface and claimed the stool across from Alex.

"Thanks." Alex sipped the beer Shannon had poured for her. Her friend was well aware that Alex's preferred beverage didn't come in a bottle with a Napa Valley label.

"What's going on, Alex?" Shannon curled her fingers around the stem of her glass but didn't partake. She liked to get straight to the heart of any matter, whether business or pleasure, before distracting herself with food or drink.

"Can't a girl visit her best friend just for the fun of it?" To wash down the lie a little better, she took a long drink.

"It's like that, is it?" Shannon joined her, turning up her own glass to bolster her courage.

Shannon was one of the strongest people Alex knew but she had a definite distaste for the unknown.

Alex had worried all the way over here as to how much she should tell Shannon. She didn't want to endanger her friend, but she needed someone to confide in. Someone who could look at this with a little more perspective than Alex was capable of just now. Someone who'd known her her whole life and could measure whether she was reading way too much between the lines here.

She'd decided to spill the beans. If she was crazy she needed someone to tell her. Unlike Patton, she could talk to Shannon without worrying that she would launch an investigation of her own. Patton would stir the stink and trouble would end up landing on him. That was the risk she wasn't sure she could take just now.

"Remember the suicide I cleaned up the other day? Charlie Crane?"

Shannon nodded before taking another drink from her glass.

"I found this thing."

Alex didn't beat around the bush. She gave Shannon the whole story, from Henson's call to her concern that someone had riffled through her things. Shannon listened, not once interrupting her.

"Order up!" Bobby called as he strode into the kitchen carrying his tray of freshly grilled steaks. The smell was heavenly. Alex's stomach rumbled.

"Let's eat while I mull this over," Shannon suggested.

She wouldn't get any argument from Alex.

They ate slowly, enjoying the good food. Shannon made the best salads with all the right greens and little flourishes that not only looked nice but proved healthier for the consumer. It was the part of that whole Type A thing.

Dinner conversation consisted of the renovations Shannon had decided she needed to do to the house now that they were empty nesters. Bobby grumbled good-naturedly after her every proposed idea for changes. Shannon basically ignored him, knowing she'd get her way in the end. Alex liked watching their easy banter. More often than not they completed each other's sentences.

Alex found herself wondering if she would wake up one of these days and regret that she didn't have anyone to be that way with. Henson's image immediately loomed large in her head. She ordered herself to stop it. She'd made her choices and she had no reason to regret anything so far.

"Did you take care of that flat tire?"

The first question out of Shannon's mouth surprised Alex. With all that she'd told her, she'd expected something a little more urgent than whether or not she'd fixed the flat. It was still in the back of her SUV.

"I haven't had time." Geez, she'd only discovered it a few hours ago. Too much had happened since to think about stopping by a service station.

"Bobby, would you mind taking care of Alex's flat?" Shannon smiled for her husband, probably promising him a special treat later.

That was another thing Alex had noticed about couples who stayed together over the long haul. Life was a series of give-and-take.

Choosing to remain single ensured that Alex got

to do the taking without worrying about the giving. Chalk one up for her side.

"Sure thing." Bobby scooted back from the table. "You pick up a nail somewhere?" he asked Alex.

"Guess so." Maybe she'd run over something in Morningside near the site of the explosion.

"You girls chill. I'll take care of the dishes later," Bobby promised his wife.

When he'd gone, Alex winked at Shannon. "Is he bucking for some special one-on-one attention later?"

"He can dream on," Shannon scoffed.

Alex recognized the pink in her cheeks. Old Shannon had every intention of giving Bobby whatever he wanted, no matter how much she denied it.

"First of all," Shannon began, "I think you should share all you know with Detective Patton regardless. Taking risks is his job. That's why he's a cop."

Alex wasn't ready to commit to that route just yet. "I'll think about it."

"You're going to have to take some added precautions at home. This could be dangerous, Alex." She put her hand on Alex's. "This guy Blake could be a killer."

Alex sighed. "That's what I've been thinking."

Though he hadn't felt like a killer. She would hate to think she'd been attracted to a killer.

"There's always the chance Timothy O'Neill is some sort of nutcase," Shannon offered, hitting on a possibility that hadn't entered Alex's mind.

"I suppose that's possible, but I'm banking on the idea that Henson wouldn't have used a nutcase for any kind of analysis, official or unofficial."

Shannon flared her hands, showing her palms. "I'll give you that one. Still, he may have made some sort of mistake, like blowing up his own house. This whole crazy story may be about covering his ass. Maybe Henson's accident really was an accident."

Alex had to admit, Shannon made some valid points. Points she hadn't even considered. "All right." Why put this off any longer? Shannon was right. Patton was a cop. His job included risking his life to solve crime. "I'll talk to Patton. I'll give him the whole story, even the part about Timothy." She took a deep breath. "Give him the lens. Leave it in his lap and let the authorities handle it."

Shannon reached for the wine bottle. "I think that's the right decision."

Alex poured herself another beer. "Hey, did I tell you about the support group Marg has joined?"

Before Alex could continue Bobby trotted back into the house via the garage door, a concerned look on his face. "Alex, you made any new enemies lately?"

Both women looked up. "What do you mean?" Alex asked, confused.

"That's not funny," Shannon chastised.

"I'm not trying to be funny," he told his wife. "Usually when you get a flat tire it means you ran over something that punctured the tread or maybe the valve went bad, but neither of those things happened."

"Give it to us in layman's terms," Shannon ordered with a puff of impatience.

"Someone opened the valve and let the air out of your tire, Alex." Bobby set his hands on his hips and, just in case they didn't get it, added, "On purpose."

CHAPTER 9

By dawn Alex had made up her mind not to wait any longer. She would tell Patton the whole story. She would keep the contact lens hidden for now as a sort of backup plan. She'd only give up that evidence if Patton couldn't move forward in his investigation without it.

Though she'd done so last night, Alex went through room after room of her home and checked the windows and doors. She couldn't remember a time when she'd been afraid in this house and she wasn't really scared now, but she did need to ensure that she took extra precautions. As independent as she was, she was no fool. Someone had definitely been inside her house.

She didn't like that one bit.

Marg was a fanatic about keeping her windows and doors locked. Alex wondered if her obsession with protecting herself had anything to do with her marriage. Those years hadn't been easy and Alex was certain she didn't know the worst of it.

She checked her reflection once more before heading out to try to catch Patton before he got into a case. Mint-green summer-weight slacks, white spaghetti strap tank with a darker green shirt with capped sleeves on top. The wedge-heeled sandals sported the same two shades of green as well as a scattering of red to tie in with the red scarf belt she'd slung around her hips.

Clothes were a major weakness. She liked pushing the boundaries of fashion. How many times had she noticed an outfit very similar to something she'd put together months prior featured in the latest issue of *Glamour* or *InStyle?* Maybe she should have gone into fashion design. But that would have required the degree she'd refused to stay in college for.

As she said before that just hadn't worked out.

So she exercised her creative side in her everyday attire. Just because she earned her living doing what most would consider a man's job, didn't mean she wasn't all girl. She'd long ago decided she was an assortment of paradoxes. Guy name, guy job, guy sense of independence and a nice set of brass ones when she needed them. None of that took away from her femininity.

With her red faux silk bag draped over her shoulder she headed for the station. Henson had mentioned on numerous occasions that he and his partner got to work by seven-thirty each morning to enjoy a couple of cups of coffee and to discuss their thoughts about ongoing cases. She was banking on the idea that Patton would stick with old habits no matter that his partner was dead and that he was a new father.

She didn't like admitting how paranoid Bobby and Shannon had made her over the deal with her tire. Shannon had insisted that she check her tires before going anywhere. Bobby gave his own advice, as well: Look for any draining under her SUV when she backed out of a parking spot in case her brake lines had been tampered with.

Nothing like starting the day off worrying whether someone wanted her dead badly enough to sneak into her yard and meddle with the functionality of her vehicle.

Just a week ago she'd climbed into her 4Runner with no concern other than an empty tank of gas. Then again, with the price of fuel soaring, that could be a pretty scary thing.

Tires were in order. She crouched down and surveyed the concrete under her vehicle. As clean as it had been when she'd parked there last night.

She checked the backseat and cargo area before clicking the remote and climbing in.

Jeez, who would have thought that preparing to drive to work could be as involved as selecting her outfit for the day?

The Miami climate had already set itself to smoldering. Alex adjusted the air-conditioning in her SUV and backed out of her driveway.

At this time of day her neighborhood was still quiet. Another hour and the whole community would be out rushing to work or to the beach.

Even with the air turned to max, she powered her window down and let the saltwater breeze flow into her vehicle. As foolish as it might sound she loved the smell of the city. The heat and salt and varied odors of activity, good and bad. That was one of her favorite parts of living in Miami. The exhilarating pulse that thumped 24-7. Life was always happening in Miami.

But so was death.

She had several cleanups on the schedule today, including four deaths. Two were natural causes, bodies already claimed, and two others were from questionable circumstances that wouldn't be available for removal until after lunch.

Brown would take the first two scenes while the Professor whittled away at the list of other jobs, including the removal of decaying vegetables stacked in a far north side duplex. Apparently the perishables had been stolen from a local warehouse, then abandoned in the rented home of one of the perpetrators.

Imagine a truckload of rotting lettuce, potatoes and tomatoes. Very messy. Like people, decaying vegetables attracted a variety of predatory insects.

Just as Henson had told her, Patton was already at the station. Alex found him in the lounge getting what he announced was his third cup of coffee for the morning.

"Morning, Jackson." He stirred two packets of sugar into his coffee. "You working a case with us this morning?"

Any time a death had to be investigated, Alex checked in with the detective in charge before beginning her cleanup. SOP. Standard operating procedure. She followed the rules. That was one of the reasons she was in this predicament in the first place.

"I came in to talk to you." She didn't mention the

subject matter since anyone could walk in at any time. She needed privacy for this. "Can we talk somewhere?" Most of the detectives shared the bull pen, but there were a few private offices and a conference room or two. A senior detective like Patton would have access to a more nonpublic setting.

"Sure." He gestured to the coffeemaker. "Coffee?"

"No thanks." Her stomach was already in knots, she didn't need any caffeine.

Patton led her across the bull pen to a small conference room. It wasn't large enough to hold the morning briefings, but for a discussion between an intimate few on a shared case it would be quite sufficient. A whiteboard and conference capable phone, along with a table that seated eight, made up the basic furnishings.

When she'd settled into a seat, Patton did the same. "So, what's up?"

She thought about the way he'd rushed away from the memorial service yesterday and she couldn't help wondering if he'd been called away for a new development related to Henson's accident or the explosion at the O'Neill home. Only one way to find out.

"Are there any new developments on Henson's accident?"

His guard went up. The transition was palpable. Visible tension tightened his facial expression and stiffened his posture.

"You keep asking me about the accident." Even his voice had changed. "Why is that, Alex?"

She braced herself and took the plunge. "The eyeball I found at the Crane scene had a contact lens attached to it. I told you that already but I don't think you considered it important. The fact is, I called Henson and he came back by the scene to pick it up just in case it was relevant."

"To the scene of Crane's suicide?" Patton suggested.

"Yes." She didn't have to see the wariness in his eyes to know how this sounded. He already didn't believe there was a problem and she'd scarcely given him the details. Cutting him some slack, she had waffled considerably on her story. But she was through with that. "Henson seemed pretty excited about it. That is why he called me that night. He said he'd taken the lens to a friend for unofficial analysis and that it appeared to be some sort of computer chip or something. Like I told you before he was really hyped."

"His friend was one Timothy O'Neill?"

She sure hadn't seen that one coming. "Yes. The kid whose house blew up."

Patton stared at his coffee but appeared to think better of further indulgence. "Jackson, we've been had."

Confusion drew her eyebrows together in a way she hated since the expression surely contributed to the lines she didn't want to form. "I'm not sure I know what you mean."

"Henson was a bit of a computer buff. He and O'Neill met a couple years ago at some sort of geek group. Let me emphasize here," Patton said, pinning her with a firm look, "this O'Neill kid is not a legitimate source for police business."

Alex nodded. "Henson told me that the analysis was unofficial."

"Anyway," Patton went on, "Timothy O'Neill turned himself in late yesterday."

About ten seconds elapsed before the full impact of his words penetrated deeply enough to evoke a response. "Turned himself in?" She had to tread carefully here. Patton could be fishing. "Wasn't he supposed to be dead?"

"We'd already confirmed that the body pulled from the rubble wasn't him. We just didn't know who or why. Apparently Timothy couldn't live with his conscience and he turned himself in."

"Did he tell you why his house blew up?" It seemed

logical to her that he would do that. The kid feared for his life.

"He told me what he told you," Patton allowed. "Then he confessed he'd made the whole thing up to throw attention away from his own guilt in what really happened."

Alex didn't get it. "What guilt? Someone tried to kill him."

Patton gave up on resisting the coffee and drank long and deep before continuing. "The explosion was an accident. He was afraid he'd be blamed for his friend's death so he made up the story he told you just in case you were to go to the police with what you knew about Henson's visit to him."

"You're saying he used Henson's accident for an alibi?"

"In a manner of speaking." Another long draw from the foam cup. "Desperate people do desperate things, Jackson. No surprise there."

"But what about the contact lens he analyzed for Henson? O'Neill insisted it contained government data." This didn't make sense. O'Neill had been terrified when he gave her back that contact lens.

"He made it up. The contact lens was just a contact lens. It blew up along with his house."

Alex tensed. "Where is he now?" O'Neill had lied. He'd given the lens back to her. But why turn himself in and then lie?

"We have him in custody. He waived his right to call an attorney. We'll keep him here, maybe get a psych eval done, until we can sort out this whole mess."

Her head was swimming with all the arguments she wanted to throw back at Patton but none of it mattered. O'Neill had confessed to blowing up his house. He'd insisted that everything he told Alex was a lie.

"I was going to call you this morning," Patton explained. "Losing Henson has been tough. O'Neill's stupid game only made bad matters worse."

That didn't explain Blake. "There's something else." She told him about the stranger who'd waited next to her SUV after the memorial service. She reminded him that she's asked him about Blake when they talked on the phone last. "If O'Neill was lying, who is this Blake character? He claimed he was investigating Henson's accident."

Patton turned his hands palm sides up. "He's lying to you. The question is why. If you'll give me a description of him and his car, I'll see what I can find."

"Wait." This just wasn't right. "I went back to the

scene of Crane's suicide. The whole place was like a setup for a life that wasn't being lived." She told him about all the unused items.

He leaned forward, set his coffee on the table. "Jackson, I've been a cop for a long time. If you really want to find trouble it's always there. Henson's death stunned us all. The way some of us deal with it is by denying the facts. We prefer to believe otherwise. Think about it. Focusing on the idea that he was murdered keeps you from having to face the reality that he's dead."

That was the end of that conversation. Patton wasn't going to buy anything she had to say. He wouldn't let her see O'Neill. She'd wasted her time coming to him.

At least she knew where she stood with the cops on the case.

Henson had been murdered.

And no one was going to find out why.

No one, unless it was her.

Her determination increasing as she exited the building, she came to an immediate stop when she saw Blake waiting near her 4Runner.

Her first instinct was to run back inside and get Patton, but then something else kicked in. The mere sight of him ignited her fury, propelling her forward once more. Somehow he was deeply involved in this whole investigation gone awry.

"The police aren't going to believe you, Alex."

"Tell me something I don't know." She wanted to tell him to kiss off and then just drive away. But he was her only connection to everything Patton opted to deny. "Who the hell are you?"

He pushed his hands into his navy designer trousers. "I've already introduced myself, Alex. You have my card. Why don't we move past the formalities and get to the heart of the matter. Your friend is dead and you want to know why. I can't help you unless you help me."

He wanted the lens or chip or whatever the hell it was.

She went for the whole dumb blonde gig. "How could I possibly help you?"

"Mr. O'Neill has taken himself out of the game for the moment. He doesn't have to worry about running anymore. All he has to do now is sit back and let the police protect him." Blake took a step closer to her. "I'm betting he gave you the item that started all his trouble in the first place."

He was one cocky SOB. "You know what?" She

took that final step, went toe-to-toe with him. As angry as she was, some part of her acknowledged that he smelled great. "If you're such a big deal fed you should be able to interrogate O'Neill wherever he is. Why don't you just waltz in there and ask him yourself?"

He smiled, the mocking attempt affected only one corner of his mouth. "What makes you think I haven't already?"

Patton would have told her…wouldn't he?

"Let's get this straight, Blake. You stay away from me. Stay away from my home and my car. I don't play well with bullies."

With that warning, she turned on her wedge heels and strode deliberately to the driver's side door of her vehicle. Screw this guy. She was out of here.

"Someone came into your home?"

She almost climbed into the 4Runner and drove away, but some subtle shift in his tone gave her pause. She spun to face him. "Like you don't know that already. You let the air out of my tire."

He didn't look the slightest bit abashed. "You have to admit it was a great conversation starter."

"Back off," she told him again. "I don't have whatever the hell it is you're looking for."

On some level she understood that the contact lens was all she had. The only connection to what really happened to Henson. She wasn't about to turn it over to anyone until she had some answers.

Taking her warning literally, he moved back two steps. He said nothing, but that blue gaze burned right through her, telling her far more than she wanted to know. This guy would not give up.

She opened the door and scooted behind the wheel. The sooner she was away from him the sooner she could think straight.

"One last question, Alex."

Again he'd startled her, walking around to her side of the vehicle. Damn him. She hesitated before closing her door, shouldn't have but she couldn't resist that he might give her some useful information.

"Who else has to die before you realize I'm the only one who can help you?"

Three beats passed before she could slam the door against the words that kept echoing in her head. She drove away, didn't look back.

Had that been a blatant threat? Against her? Against her mother or her friends?

Alex drove faster than she should have, mainly

because she was fiercely pissed off. How dare he threaten her!

Damn. Realization slowed her rate of speed. She hadn't checked her tires or the spot where she'd parked for any drained fluids. She pressed her brake lightly just to make sure it still worked.

Relief flooded her when the vehicle reacted as expected.

For the fifteen minutes it took her to maneuver morning rush hour traffic and get to the office, she steamed. Her fury, fueled by the idea that this guy thought he could control her, built steadily.

"Better men have tried," she muttered.

She didn't care what Patton believed. She didn't care how smart Blake thought he was. No one pushed Alex Jackson around. And she never, ever let down her friends. Henson had been a friend. She would find out what happened to him.

Brown and the Professor were already out on her calls when Alex arrived at the office. Marg was on the phone talking to a local who's who magazine about doing a write-up on Never Happened. God love her. Alex was convinced that a large portion of the company's success was because of Margie Jackson and her persuasive personality. Keep the booze and men away from her and she was amazing. Get her tied up in a physical relationship and she dived back into the bottle…headfirst.

One look at Shannon's face and Alex knew the day was only going to get worse.

"What happened?"

Shannon gave her one of those looks that said this was bad, very bad. "The Professor is on his way back here. He got to the dead veggie scene and almost crashed through the building."

Alex felt her brow furrow with the precursor to tomorrow's wrinkles. "What do you mean? Was he hurt?"

"No, he's fine, but the brakes in the truck aren't. They failed, Alex. The Professor almost crashed because of it. The mechanic who came and towed the truck away just called. Some brake line was damaged and slowly leaked out all the fluid causing the failure."

A chill sank all the way to Alex's bones. "Have that mechanic check out all of our vehicles, one by one. I want to be sure this doesn't happen again."

Shannon nodded and reached for the phone.

As Alex headed for her office, over her shoulder she called, "When the Professor gets here I need to talk to the two of you. Get Marg to man the phones."

The next half hour Alex spent taking a stab at catching up. Wasn't going to happen, but she kept promising herself she'd get all those reports done eventually. Eventually being the key word.

She hated trying to catch up but it kept her mind off what had happened with the truck. God, it could have been so much worse. Timothy O'Neill's warning echoed in her brain. *You should disappear, Alex. Or you could end up dead, too.*

Thankfully the Professor arrived and he and Shannon rescued her from diving into that reality alone.

Alex shored up her courage with a bolstering breath. "O'Neill turned himself in to the police." The next two minutes were spent bringing the Professor up to speed on what had taken place during the past forty-eight hours. "No one is going to consider Henson's death a murder unless I can prove that O'Neill's original story is the real story. O'Neill warned me that I could be in danger and now we know he was right." The idea that the Professor could have been killed in that truck twisted her guts into knots.

"Let's take a step back," the Professor suggested, his demeanor remaining calm despite his adventure this morning.

Alex gave him her undivided attention. God knew she wasn't sure what to do from here.

"This began with a suicide. Charles Crane. That is where you should begin."

"I went back to his place," she said, only just realizing that she hadn't told either of them about what she'd found. Shannon's eyes grew rounder as Alex shared what she'd discovered at Crane's place.

"A cover life."

Both she and Shannon stared at the Professor questioningly.

"Spies, undercover agents, men and women in those professions often live a shadow life to accomplish their mission. It's not who they really are, sometimes they scarcely scratch the surface of living it. But this other life serves a purpose, usually as a protection of their true identity. Clearly Charles Crane was not who he appeared to be. Just as nothing that has occurred since his death has turned out to be what it appears."

"That's how it felt," Alex agreed, thinking back on what she'd seen. "The house looked as if it was being lived in, but it was all for show."

"This could be dangerous. We can't prove someone tampered with the Professor's brake line, but under the circumstances I'd say that's a damned likely possibility," Shannon tossed out. "Alex isn't a cop or a spy. She could be getting herself into something that could get her killed. It could get all of us killed."

Alex shuddered at the idea that this whole crazy situation had already endangered her friends.

The Professor nodded. "That's why she must do the last thing they would expect."

Alex didn't even try to speculate what he meant.

"Allow Blake to believe you're cooperating. Since he's the only contact you have, we'll start with him. Meanwhile we figure out who Charlie Crane was and why he died. Once we know who he was, things may become much more apparent. At the very least we'll have gained some leverage."

Alex looked from her lifelong friend to her newer but equally cherished friend. "Henson is dead. O'Neill was almost killed. You," she said to the Professor, "could have been killed this morning. Are you two sure you want to be involved in this thing?"

"I resent that you would even ask," Shannon snipped.

"I, as well," the Professor seconded.

As much as she worried that this investigation

would bring harm to them, it felt damned good to have someone on her side in this.

"So I should contact Blake and lead him to believe I'm ready to cooperate?"

"There's an old saying, Alex," the Professor offered sagely. "Keep your friends close—"

"And your enemies closer," she finished for him.

She thought about the man, Austin Blake. Keeping him close wouldn't be such a hardship.

As long as it didn't get her killed.

CHAPTER 10

Alex missed lunch again.

She'd gotten a call from a lady who needed an estimate on getting an unsightly mess cleaned up ASAP. She indicated there was blood and other things but hedged whenever Alex asked for additional details. She insisted she would pay a bonus if the job could be completed today.

Alex's suspicions automatically kicked into high gear. Anyone who avoided the details and offered to pay a bonus usually had something to hide. Not that it was necessarily a criminal act. Might have been totally unintentional.

People did that sometimes. Accidentally killed a loved one—it sounded unlikely she knew but it did happen—and then they were afraid to call the police. Alex would end up having to make the call for him or her while he or she sobbed hysterically about how he or she hadn't meant to hurt anyone. Most of the time she chose to believe the story. The explanations were too bizarre to be made up.

Alex felt reasonably certain this one would fall into that category considering the amount of blood the woman talked about. She hadn't sounded hysterical but there had been an odd tension simmering beneath her calm. Only one way to find out. The woman clearly needed assistance of some sort.

The temperature in her 4Runner—she meticulously checked the tires and undercarriage before heading out—took forever to cool down. The midday sun had turned the closed-up interior into an oven. If there was a body at this scene she hoped the house was air-conditioned.

She made the necessary turns and then cruised along the specified street, watching for the house number of her potential client. Kids played in the yards, toys cluttering what was otherwise a neatly trimmed landscape surrounding equally neat cookie-cutter houses.

The home of the woman who'd called was a different story, however. Chipped, peeling paint that screamed for attention. A tangle of overgrown grass, more brown than green as a result of the heat and continued negligence. The dented garage door was closed, the driveway was cracked and crumbling. Not exactly home sweet home.

A middle-aged woman came out onto the porch as Alex climbed out of her SUV. She waved a hello. "I'm Alex Jackson of Never Happened." Alex gestured to her vehicle. "I have to grab a few things but I'll be right in."

"I don't want you to do anything until I have an estimate," the woman, who was hopefully Janet Bell, reminded.

Alex nodded her understanding and went around to the cargo door to prepare for entering the house. Since she didn't know what to expect outside blood, she pulled on shoe covers and gloves.

"You're Mrs. Bell?" Alex asked as she climbed the steps leading to the porch.

"Yes." Janet dragged in a heavy breath. "Prepare yourself, Miss Jackson, this is not a pretty sight."

Alex gifted her with a comforting smile. "Trust me, Mrs. Bell, it won't be anything I haven't seen before."

Mrs. Bell managed a tight smile. "This way."

Alex followed her inside. Air-conditioned. Good. But even the coolness of the interior couldn't disguise the smell of blood. Coppery, goose-bump inspiring.

No matter how often she walked into a scene and encountered the same bodily fluids, there was something about blood that made her shiver.

They passed through the living room and moved down the dimly lit hall. Mrs. Bell hesitated outside what was probably a bedroom door. "I apologize in advance for this immoral image. Please don't associate what you're about to see with me." She moved her head solemnly from side to side. "This has nothing to do with me."

Alex kept that smile of reassurance tacked in place. "Why don't you stay out here while I have a look? There's no reason for you to go in again."

Mrs. Bell nodded jerkily.

Alex reached for the door but hesitated. As sorry as she felt for the lady there was one thing she had to know. "Mrs. Bell." She turned to look at the poor woman. "Is there anything in here that merits calling the police? I wouldn't want to contaminate a crime scene."

Her eyes rounded like saucers. "Oh, I couldn't have the police coming in and seeing this. I'll call them as soon as you've taken care of…" She motioned toward the still unopened door. "When you've done what you have to do, I'll call whomever I need to." Her shoulders squared with determination. "I couldn't possibly bear the humiliation of having the media vultures get wind of this. If the police are called, the media, as you know, will come, too."

This was not good. Evidently this woman understood that whatever was in this room required the participation of the police. Alex couldn't make her call, but, once she'd viewed the scene, she could damn sure call herself.

Alex opened the door and a blast of metallic odor—coagulated blood—hit her in the face. Her empty stomach roiled in protest. Not even the smell she hated could detract from the stark amazement at what she saw.

A man, fifty-five or sixty she guessed, was hanging from the ceiling fan in the middle of the room. There wasn't more than two inches of space between the tip of his toes and the worn blue fabric from the chair directly behind him that he had apparently stepped off.

At first glance it looked as if the man had committed suicide. Not only had he hung himself, he'd somehow managed to cut an artery in his neck. But then the other details came into focus. Like the careful padding around the rope's noose and the loose way his hands were bound in front of him by the silk scarf. Both the noose's padding and the scarf were soaked in blood.

The straight razor with which he'd attempted to cut the noose had fallen onto the floor near an open magazine. At least he'd died happy it seemed, considering the sultry vixen so vividly exposed on the magazine's centerfold.

For a few seconds more Alex tried to figure out why he hadn't just kicked around until his toes found the chair? Then he certainly could have reached above his head and held on to the rope to take the pressure off his neck. Maybe cutting himself loose was another part of the excitement. She'd heard how some folks got off on the whole danger element of asphyxiation, but the knife was over the top. Most claimed that asphyxia made the orgasm better, out of this world even. Some sexual partners strangled each other to achieve the effect.

Personally Alex preferred her orgasms the old-fashioned way. Not that she was a prude or anything. She was happy to try new techniques, as long as they didn't involve a close encounter with death.

No matter how embarrassing the situation, Alex had no choice but to bring in the police. From what she saw she'd stake her reputation that the guy's death was accidental, but she wasn't the official who could make that call.

She backed out of the room and closed the door, removed her gloves and turned to face the dead man's wife. "Mrs. Bell, I'm sorry but the police will have to be called first. This is an unattended death and to clean it up before they've had a look would be breaking the law."

Horror laid claim to the woman's expression. "But I don't understand. He's done this a hundred times and lived to laugh about it. How could he be so stupid?"

The idea that she knew what her husband was up to wasn't as startling as the idea that his death didn't appear to be paramount just now.

"I'm sorry for your loss, Mrs. Bell. I'm sure you're suffering from shock. Losing a spouse is particularly shattering. Why don't you—"

"A spouse!" She looked even more mortified if that was possible. "He's not my husband. He's my brother! I can't have this getting out."

Well, no wonder she was so pissed off. It was bad enough when a spouse dragged his or her better half into an ugly situation, but a brother should keep something like this to himself.

As the woman said, the dumb bastard had probably done this hundreds of times without a glitch. Most likely he'd gotten a little too confident about his skill at escaping death. Maybe he'd added the knife to ensure the same rush. Like a drug addict, he may have wanted to add another layer of danger.

"I tell you what," Alex heard herself say, "you sit with me in the living room and I'll call a detective friend of mine. He'll come over without calling it in right away." The media vultures, as Janet called them, kept their ears peeled on all police frequencies. If the event were called in, the media would come.

"Thank you so much, Miss Jackson."

Alex patted the woman's arm. "Not a problem."

Why the hell did men not think about the ramifications of their actions before they went totally stupid? And who usually ended up cleaning up the mess and facing the music afterward? Women.

Thank God she'd stayed single. Thank God her mother hadn't had any other children, she added as an afterthought.

She didn't have to worry about some guy doing this to her.

Alex entered the number for Patton's mobile. He

didn't exactly owe her a favor but he would come if she asked.

She realized something about her interaction with the male species. She liked men a lot. A whole lot. But her favorite interactions with men were the ones that resulted in friendship, no matter how they'd started out. Look at her friend Cody at the morgue. They'd had a great physical thing going for a while and stayed friends. That was good. Even Henson. A pang of regret she couldn't totally dismiss sliced through her. He had made a difference in her life, had an impact. But anything more than the few dates they'd shared had been beyond what she wanted.

What was so wrong with that? Did that make her damaged somehow?

The way she saw it, a woman didn't have to stick with the same guy or marry anyone to be happy over the long haul. She had lots of companions. Just not one who lived in her house or told her what to do.

That last thought prompted an image of Austin Blake. He was exactly the type who liked to be the boss, who liked the power of having a woman answer to him.

Not her type at all.

Men like Blake were good for one thing only: an all-nighter—just once. Lots of hot, steamy sex for however many hours he could hold out and then walk away. No strings, no regrets.

Unless, of course, he proved to be a killer as well as handsome.

If Blake killed her friend, he was definitely going to regret it. He might not know it yet, since he thought he owned the world. But he would know. Very soon.

Alex dropped by her house after waiting with Janet Bell until Detective Patton had arrived. She had promised to return for cleanup the moment the police released the scene.

She probably should have gone back to the office but she felt the need to shower and change. No doubt Janet had felt the same upon walking in to find her brother hanging from the ceiling fan.

While they'd waited for Patton to arrive, Janet had told Alex about how she checked on her brother regularly. He'd never married and she worried that his sex fetishes had likely held him back. Alex didn't comment. She'd bet the same. In her experience guys who needed those kinds of extreme measures to get off were never satisfied with normal physical intimacies.

Alex shuddered as she peeled off her clothes. If she were a shrink she'd want to delve into the guy's past to find out what had caused him to feel the need for a near-death experience every time he ejaculated. But she wasn't a shrink. She did, however, feel sorry for the guy's sister.

She stood very still for a moment. He was just like the other victims she'd encountered lately…alone. If his sister hadn't checked up on him, how long would it have been before anyone missed him?

Did choosing to live alone mean she'd end up that way? Discovered dead in the bathtub or in bed by some friend or neighbor?

She suddenly wondered who had discovered Henson? Had he lain dead or dying in his car for hours before anyone noticed?

Why was it that being alone suddenly felt so lonesome?

Alex's cell rang and she jerked at the unexpected sound. She turned on the shower so the water would warm up, then grabbed her phone.

"Alex Jackson."

"We have a problem, Alex Jackson."

Her free hand struggling with the clasp of her bra, Alex stilled. She didn't recognize the voice but that wasn't what sent the chill through her. It was the innately cruel tone that instantly made her understand this was not a former customer calling to complain.

"Who is this?" She reached for a robe, abruptly feeling exposed.

"A friend of Charlie Crane's."

She held the phone back from her ear to see if a number showed on the caller ID display. Too late. The only thing it showed right now was *talk*.

Resting the phone against her ear once more, she cautiously resumed the conversation. "I'm afraid you'll need to call Detective Jimmy Patton of Miami Beach PD or the morgue for any information regarding the body of your late friend."

Silence.

Alex licked her lips and held her breath just to make sure he didn't pick up on any unsteadiness in her.

"It's not the body I'm looking for, Miss Jackson. I think you know that."

She initiated a long, slow breath before responding. "Any personal effects left behind can be obtained from—"

"Miss Jackson, let's not play games."

"What do you want?" she demanded, allowing him to hear the annoyance that flared. His irritating monotone was getting on her nerves. Who the hell was this jerk? Obviously someone who wanted the lens. Maybe one of Blake's cronies?

"You have something that belonged to Mr. Crane," he said with total confidence. "I must have it."

"Look, buddy"—no way was she admitting a damned thing—"I don't know what the hell you're talking about and I'm just about sick of you guys throwing your weight around."

"Ah. You've met Mr. Blake, I presume."

Well, duh. "I've made his acquaintance."

"Watch your back with Mr. Blake, Miss Jackson. He's a very dangerous man. You wouldn't like him if you knew all the facts."

"Who says I like him now?" She suddenly wished her phone had a record option. Why was it all this crazy shit happened when no one else was around to see or hear it?

"There are things you don't know."

"You're right there," she snapped. "Like who killed my friend."

"Yes."

She could almost see this jerk nodding his head as if she were a slow learner under his tutelage.

"Detective Henson. You want to know who killed him."

"Was it you?" Hey, why beat around the bush?

"I'm afraid you'll have to ask Mr. Blake about what happened to Detective Henson. My only concern is the contact lens you have in your possession."

Her gaze narrowed and her temper flared. "Since you're probably the one who's been going through my things I would think you'd know I *don't* have it." Asshole. She understood that she wasn't thinking rationally right now but she rarely did when she got this angry. And all the rationality in the world wouldn't change how badly she wanted to kick this guy in the teeth.

"We need to discuss this matter, Miss Jackson. It is of the utmost importance that I reclaim the item. I will gladly tell you everything you want to know about Blake and the danger he represents for you if you'll meet me face-to-face."

"Like I'm going to meet you." Please, what did he take her for?

"Name the place, Miss Jackson. The more public the better. I will be happy to meet on your terms."

Well now, that put a whole different spin on things. If she could pick the time and place, she was all over it. She had questions for this guy.

"All right then." The more she knew about Blake

the better she could handle what was to come. And even if this was a setup, she needed to know this new player.

The game had already begun and she was way behind. Any leverage she could obtain was essential. She owed it to Henson.

Alex dressed for the occasion. White low-slung slacks, white scooped blouse and matching summer jacket. The powder-blue pointed-toe stilettos and leather belt were her only concessions to color.

Her maternal grandmother's advice on the topic had always stayed with her. Always dress your best, she would tell Alex, on two occasions in particular: when you were going to the bank for a loan so they would know you're good for it; and, whenever you go to the doctor. Alex remembered asking her why she should dress up if she felt sick enough to go to the doctor. Her grandmother would tell her sagely, "So they'll think you're worth saving."

Well, this wasn't the bank or the doctor's office, but the idea was the same. She wanted this guy to know that he was dealing with a woman fully capable of meeting whatever challenge he tossed her way.

Besides she always liked to look especially good

when she went to the mall. It was impossible to go and not see someone she knew. An old friend from high school or a man she'd dated. Miami was full of guys she'd dated once or twice. Good thing there was a steady flow of new ones moving into town every day.

Life never got boring in Miami.

While she waited near the fountain she contemplated all she knew about Henson's death. Not that much. Only that one phone call he'd made to her and what O'Neill had told her. But that was enough. It didn't take a degree in psychology or criminology to know why he'd told the story he had. He'd been made. The cops knew the body they'd removed from his house wasn't him. The only way he could possibly hope to protect himself was by being incarcerated just as Blake said.

The whole idea of being in danger over that stupid contact lens still felt surreal.

But Henson was dead. Timothy O'Neill's home was a pile of rubble and his friend was dead. Whatever this was, it was bad and it was big.

Her main objective with this meeting was to get a visual ID of this new player and to determine if he was a good guy or a bad one. What she learned about him, considering his opinion of Blake, would help her come to more accurate conclusions about both men.

Alex checked the time on her cell and surveyed the crowd mingling around in the mall's main thoroughfare. Lots of people. She wasn't afraid. He couldn't touch her here without being caught by mall security. At least two security guards hung out close to the fountain at all times. To prevent potential thieves interested in grabbing a handful of the coins glittering at the bottom of the lovely fountain pool. She waved at one of the guards. They'd dated years ago. He was married now, but they were still friends.

Her senses went on edge as a distinguished gentleman of about sixty moved toward her. Charcoal suit, gray hair, confident stride. Hands right where she could see them and thankfully empty.

"Miss Jackson," he acknowledged as he moved up beside her at the fountain's south side.

"Mr…" She frowned dramatically. "I don't think I got your name."

"My name is not important."

Of course it wasn't. Why hadn't she thought of that line? She'd heard it in at least three movies.

"Sorry, pal." She backed away a step. "I don't talk to strangers."

Urgency and no small amount of irritation claimed his expression. "My name is Marshall Avery."

"All right, Mr. Avery"—she folded her arms over her chest—"I want to know what this whole thing is about."

He smiled. She was certain it was meant to be pleasant or charming but it wasn't. "It's about a technology war, Miss Jackson. Our country is losing, save for a few very special projects. The contact lens Crane was wearing is a prototype. If it falls into the wrong hands…" He heaved a monumental breath. "We're already far behind on too many fronts. We need this development."

"Why was Crane wearing it?" If it was so top secret and so important, what was a guy like Crane doing with it in Miami?

"Crane was one of our test subjects. A ghost living among Miami's citizens, overlooked and ignored. The feedback he and the handful of others participating in these tests provide is invaluable to the technology's success. It is imperative that this unfortunate accident not destroy the whole program."

She had to admit that what he said made some sense. "If Crane was so important to the program why would he kill himself?" He had to know how important it was to protect the lens. Why jeopardize something this important?

"We believe he was murdered."

"Why didn't the murderer take the lens?" He had to give her more than that.

"We can only assume that he was unfamiliar with the design we'd selected for Crane. The various venues of this technology are a closely guarded secret."

"What exactly is the technology?" Might as well go for the gold. Her curiosity hadn't been this high since she'd made out with Frankie Barker under the bleachers at her old high school's football field.

"I'm sure you know I can't share that information." His smile was a bit more sincere this time. "If you have the lens I must reclaim it. There is no reason for this to burden you further. I'm certain you realize how dangerous this could prove."

She was relatively certain she'd just been threatened.

"First, I'll need the rest of the information on Blake you promised. You did say everything. Then we can discuss where the lens might be." No way was she admitting that she had it just yet.

His eyes tapered with suspicion. "Are you saying you don't have the lens?"

He was fishing. He or his associate hadn't found it in her home so he was trying to intimidate her into an answer. She'd been right to be overly suspicious of this guy when he'd called. Thank God she'd had the foresight to properly prepare.

"If you're not going to hold up your end of this bargain," she argued, "we have nothing else to discuss."

"You're on the verge of making a very serious mistake, Miss Jackson. I would suggest you do all within your power to get the lens back to me in a timely manner. You won't find anyone else who can protect you from Blake."

"What about Blake?" He'd told her that Blake was not to be trusted. She wanted to know exactly who Blake was. "Are you telling me he's an enemy of this country? That he'd steal our technology to sell to someone else for his own benefit?" Wouldn't that make him a terrorist? "And how do I know you're not after the same thing?"

His eyes turned cold and hard with impatience. His right hand slid into his jacket pocket. "Miss Jackson, I have a 9 mm Beretta in my pocket. I don't want to have to use it, but believe me, I won't hesitate if the necessity arises. Let's take a walk so that we may discuss the subject further without any interference."

Alex studied his pocket where his hand now rested. There could be a gun in there. Her heart had started to beat a little faster, pumping adrenaline through her veins. She couldn't help Henson if she got herself dead. But she couldn't give this guy what he wanted without knowing who the hell he was and who the hell Blake was. She refused to let Henson's death be for nothing.

"I can prove Blake killed your detective friend," the man insisted, "but first you must come with me. It's for your own safety."

"If you can prove who killed my friend, then we have something to talk about," she allowed, "but we'll do it on my terms."

Avery's face reddened with the rage seeping out around his rigid composure. "You'll come with me now unless you want to become one of Miami's sad statistics."

Alex refused to let fear get the better of her. She nodded toward the upper gallery where folks on the second level walked past. "You see the gentleman wearing the bow tie up there?"

Avery glanced briefly in the direction she'd indicated.

"He's got his finger on speed dial for 911. Down

here there are two guards less than fifty feet away who're watching every move we make. One of 'em's a friend of mine. How do you want this to end, Mr. Avery?" She went on when he made no move to answer. "All I want is the truth. I want whoever killed my friend to pay and I want your precious technology to end up back where it belongs. You can either help me accomplish that or you can do what you will and take your chances on surviving."

Instead of responding he did the last thing she'd expected.

He wheeled around and hurried away.

What the hell was that about?

Just then, in her peripheral vision, she got her answer.

Austin Blake.

CHAPTER 11

Alex didn't stick around to see how things turned out with Blake and Avery, if those were even their names. When Blake didn't slow in his pursuit of Avery as he rushed right past her, she figured she was free to go.

She'd thanked her security guard friend for helping her out before meeting with the Professor at the escalator. Twenty minutes later they had arrived back at the office. She told herself that the shakiness she felt as she climbed out of her 4Runner had nothing to do with fear and everything to do with victory, but she had a feeling that might be a lie.

Avery had scared her.

Dammit.

A great deal of who she was, okay, maybe her entire existence, was tied inextricably with her sense of independence. Being afraid didn't bode well with maintaining the level of confidence required to feel totally independent.

As Alex and the Professor pushed through the glass entry door, Shannon looked up and asked, "How'd it go?"

"That depends upon your vision of what the end result should have been," the Professor told her.

Alex tossed her purse onto the sofa and dropped next to it. "I met the guy. He said his name was Marshall Avery. He wanted the lens. Insisted it was some kind of advanced technology that would cause the end of the world if it fell into the wrong hands."

Shannon made one of those *yeah right* sounds.

"He wanted Alex to leave the mall with him," the Professor said, cutting to the part she wanted to forget as he settled into one of the chairs flanking the sofa. "He claimed to have a gun in his pocket."

"Oh my God!" Shannon's eyes were wide with a far too familiar fear. "What do you think he intended to do? Surely he wouldn't have hurt you?"

Alex turned her hands up in an I-dunno gesture. "Blake showed up and Avery took off."

The Professor's gaze bumped into hers and something in his eyes told her that what he had seen wasn't quite that simple, but he didn't argue.

"What're you going to do now?"

Alex wished she knew. All she'd gotten from Avery were more questions instead of any answers. And he wanted the lens. Desperately.

A few hours ago she'd been all cocky and determined to strong-arm the truth out of the guy. But that hadn't happened. At this moment she wasn't certain of anything, most assuredly of what she should or shouldn't do.

The police, including Patton, wouldn't listen to her when she suggested that Henson's accident had been no accident. Even O'Neill had wimped out on her. Giving the kid grace, his friends were dead and he was terrified that he would be next.

That left Alex with no avenues whatsoever other than Avery and Blake.

How the hell could this happen in real life?

Bizarre computer chips and secret agents! *Gimme a break!* This was movie and book fodder, not part of the regular workday grind. A week ago her biggest worry had been whether she'd end this dating dry spell before she set an all-time personal record.

And here she was wondering if that old guy would have killed her had she not had the foresight to arrange for a backup plan.

The idea of dying now, at forty, with so much life ahead of her...so many things she wanted to do, made her feel sick to her stomach. Henson had lost out on his entire future. Sure his career had already reached great heights but what about his other goals—like a wife and kids. He'd wanted those things and he'd missed out. If she had died today, what would she have missed out on?

That nothing came immediately to mind bothered her unreasonably. She had things to look forward to...she had friends....

Just stop it, Alex. What the hell had been wrong with her the past few days? She just couldn't get past all this intense self-reflection.

Focus. She had to stay focused. It was the only way to ever get justice for Henson's murder.

Trying to look at the situation rationally, if what Avery said was true, Crane hadn't committed suicide at all. He'd been murdered just like Henson. But that didn't make sense, either, because he'd still been wearing the contact. She didn't buy Avery's suggestion that the killer hadn't known what to look for. That would make for one dumb killer.

Why didn't the government simply come in and take what was theirs? She could only imagine the surveillance techniques they had at their disposal. Why were people merely assuming she had the lens? Why didn't they know for sure? Her home had been searched at least once. Where was that fancy technology she'd seen used in the movies? Even her ingenious hiding place shouldn't withstand fancy gadgets designed for finding hidden items.

Was that why Blake and Avery had shown up in her life? Were they supposed to watch her until they had the truth or the lens, whichever came first? Had they been hired to retrieve it at all costs?

But which one was the bad guy? Obviously they weren't working on the same team.

"Perhaps it's time to take this one to the FBI."

Alex snapped out of her troubling thoughts, surprised at the Professor's pronouncement. "But you were the one who suggested I see what Blake was really up to by cooperating to a degree."

"That was before men started wielding weaponry," he countered frankly. "A deflated tire is one thing, a faulty brake line another, but this is an entirely different ball game, Alexis. You're in over your head, I fear."

Deep down she knew he was right. Hell, he was always right. But she couldn't back off. Not now that she fully understood what would happen if she did.

The local police weren't going to take her seriously. Henson's death would never be properly investigated beyond the obvious. She couldn't let go and pretend that didn't matter. He deserved better than that. She was the only person who could see this through.

She turned her full attention to the Professor. "You're right. I am in over my head. But I can't let this go. I'll just have to be careful."

"How did I know you'd say that?" Shannon shook her head. "You always were bullheaded."

Before Alex could respond, Marg entered the lobby in a flurry of reds and golds. "You're not going to believe this," she huffed impatiently. "I crashed my Miata."

Alex was on her feet before the statement stopped reverberating in the air. "What? Are you okay?"

Marg chafed her hands up and down her arms. "I'm okay, but I was terrified there for a second." She closed her eyes and drew in a deep breath. "All I could see was the back of that bus coming closer and closer."

Alex put her arm around her mother's shoulder. "What happened?"

Marg shook her head. "I don't know. I pushed the brake, but it didn't work…just went all the way to the floorboard without doing a damned thing."

That was it. Alex had Shannon call Brown back to the office via a taxi. All the vehicles they drove would be checked again before anyone else got behind a wheel. If it took all night, so be it, they'd use rentals instead. She'd have every single vehicle checked every day, if necessary.

The Professor borrowed Patsy's shop van from next door and he and Brown headed off on a call where a landlord had found a meth lab in a house he rented. He'd already called the cops and reported the situation.

Alex dug around in her purse and pulled out the card Blake had given her. She went into her office and punched in the number; the call went straight to his voice mail. If she hadn't been so furious she would have enjoyed the deep, husky sound of his voice, but she was mad as hell. She left him a message to get back to her ASAP then closed the phone.

He had some explaining to do. She wasn't ready to call him a killer as Avery had, but she damn well intended to find out.

Then she went across the hall to the lounge to check on Marg. She was seated at her table, scanning her messages.

Alex pulled up a chair and sat down beside her.

She couldn't ever remember being more terrified than she had been when her mother had said that her brakes failed. For all the arguing they did, for all the trouble she gave Alex, she didn't want to lose her.

"You sure you're okay?"

Marg nodded, the blond ringlets hanging from her meticulously coiffed bun bounced. "I'm fine, Alex. I'm just worried about my car."

For the first time in a long time, Alex looked closely at her mother. She was a beautiful woman for her age. She was a beautiful woman for any age. The tiniest lines had started to crease the corners of her eyes. Worry lines no doubt. Alex had been there all those years when Marg and Dex Jackson had fought like cats and dogs. His constant boozing and womanizing had provided fertile fields for dissension. The marriage had been doomed from the beginning. It was an outright miracle the two had stayed together as long as they had.

"How'd your meeting go?"

Marg shot her a look. "You should come along and see for yourself."

Alex heaved a sigh. "I don't have a physical intimacy problem."

"That's right," Marg agreed. "What you have is a fear of commitment."

Oh, Jesus. Alex pushed out of her chair, gave herself the element of height. "I don't have a fear of anything," she snapped. "I simply chose not to spend my life catering to someone else's needs."

How the hell could her mother, of all people, say this?

"Alex." Marg looked up at her, her voice far too calm. Alex wanted her to be as furious as she was. "I know that your father and I did this to you." She held up a hand when Alex would have launched a verbal defense. "I'm very proud of you for being so independent and capable, but there comes a time when everybody needs somebody." Her eyes searched her daughter's. "I just don't want you to wind up alone like me. I've been watching you all these years and I know what I see. Your fear is going to cost you far more than you know. That old saying better to have loved and lost than never to have loved at all wasn't coined for nothing."

Alex didn't respond, she just went back to her own office. She had wanted to retaliate with some witty remark, but the words had hit far too close to what she'd been feeling lately for comfort.

So she did the one surefire thing to take her mind off the subject. She grabbed herself a Diet Coke and snack crackers and started plowing through the work she'd been putting off.

"I could file some of those final reports if you get around to them," Shannon said from the door. "And those invoices need to be signed off on, too."

Alex groaned. What had sounded like a good plan now felt like slave labor. God she hated reports. She stared at the pile of paperwork on her desk. Putting it off any longer would equate to negligence.

She took a swig of her drink and dived in. If she worked hard enough she wouldn't have to think about the idea that the weekend was coming and she had no date. Not even a prospect.

Going into week four was absolutely unacceptable.

No. What was really unacceptable was the idea that her mother could be right about too many things.

Alex had never been one to wait for things to come to her. Going after what she wanted was a standard she lived by. Since she didn't like cruising the club scene, she'd just have to dig out her little pink book.

Or maybe she'd call Cody and see what he was up to this weekend.

Certain her dating hiatus was coming to an end, she continued to plow through the mound of paperwork on her desk.

Pretending it would go away hadn't worked.
Neither had praying for a thief with a paper fetish.

Alex gave herself a pat on the back as she surveyed
her now amazingly neat office. She'd finished all the
reports and signed off on every single invoice. She'd
even taken the time to organize the clutter. A little
anyway. It wouldn't get her any kind of beautification
award, but at least one could walk through without
stepping on something or tripping.

Deciding that she'd accomplished more than
enough for one afternoon, she grabbed her bag and
headed for the door, turning her light off as she went.

Shannon would be proud. No, she'd be shocked.

Alex did a double take in the front office. The
Professor sat behind Shannon's desk. Before she
could ask where Shannon had gotten to, the phone
rang and the Professor answered with his own rendi-
tion of the company motto.

She assumed that if he was back so was Brown, but
he was nowhere in sight. Alex had to admit she was
a little disappointed that she'd missed whatever
fashion statement he'd made this morning. Shannon
had mentioned something about Britney Spears and
rolled her eyes.

The Professor took a message and placed the receiver back into its cradle. "Shannon had an appointment and had to leave a few minutes early."

It was past six. Alex doubted she'd left early as far as what her actual work schedule was. But she knew it was early for Shannon.

"Where's Brown?" Maybe he'd gone out on an assignment she didn't know about. Shannon probably hadn't wanted to disturb her once she'd started on the reports for fear Alex would use the excuse to move onto something else. But then that didn't feel right since Shannon never left the office without giving Alex a heads-up.

"He had an appointment."

Now she was really suspicious. Not that Brown didn't have his share of appointments, but because of the way the Professor avoided eye contact when he told what was obviously a lie.

"Oh." Alex started to leave it at that, but her curiosity wouldn't let her. "What about the cleanup with the possible meth lab?"

"Formaldehyde."

"Formaldehyde?" Why would anyone dump formaldehyde? She tried to think what drug-making processes required that particular chemical.

"The previous tenant liked preserving his pets who passed away."

An icky sensation crept over Alex. "Don't tell me he had Fido in a big glass jar."

"A lizard, a boa, two guinea pigs and one cat."

"Gross." She'd heard of people having their deceased pets stuffed, but this went to a whole new level. "Why didn't he take his animals with him?"

"Died."

A frown crossed her forehead. "How? He wasn't in the house when he croaked, was he?"

The Professor taped the phone message for Shannon on her computer monitor where she'd see it first thing in the morning. "No. At work. Apparently a member of the family was looking for a nice suit for the deceased's funeral and stumbled, literally, upon one of the large glass pickle jars."

"I'll bet that was a hell of a shock."

The Professor nodded. "He had to be taken to the E.R. His heart or maybe the fumes. The landlord insisted on having the place cleaned up immediately."

"I'm outta here," Alex said. "You should go, too."

The Professor stood. "I'll be following you home."

He would be following her home? "Why?"

The Professor stood and pushed in Shannon's chair. "Just a precaution in case Avery shows up. Shannon's husband kindly brought us one of his construction trucks to use until ours is repaired."

She didn't bother arguing. When her employees got an idea in their heads she just had to go with the flow. She'd have to remember to thank Bobby for his help with transportation.

As she drove home, glancing at the Professor at the wheel of his car in her rearview mirror, she considered that maybe Marg was wrong. Maybe Alex wouldn't die alone. She had a lot of people who cared about her.

What did she need with a husband or kids?

There she went going down that road again. What had her hung up on the whole "family" thing? Shannon's kids were off in college. There was just no reason.

Oh hell.

Maybe her biological clock had finally kicked into gear. All this time she thought she didn't have one.

What kind of crappy joke was Mother Nature playing on her?

If she were totally honest with herself she would know what the problem was. She was forty and the one guy who'd made her think about what came next had just died.

And now all she could do was wonder if there even would be a next.

It was dark when the knock echoed across Alex's living room. She'd curled up on the sofa to watch a movie.

Dammit. She set her bowl of popcorn aside and glanced down at her nightshirt. It wasn't exactly revealing but the logo on the front read, Sex Does a Body Good.

It wouldn't be her mother, she mused as she moved to the door; she would just use her key. Besides, they probably weren't speaking. Maybe Shannon had decided to drop in and check on her. Everyone, including Alex, was worried about this whole Avery-Blake thing. She'd checked her doors and windows to ensure they were all locked before settling in front of the television. And she had her pepper spray handy. She held it firmly in her right hand as she peered through the peephole in her door.

She gasped, instantly taking a wide step back.

Austin Blake stood on her porch.

For about three seconds she contemplated whether

letting him in was a good idea or not. But she had no intention of being a prisoner in her own home.

She opened the door a crack. "What do you want?"

"We need to talk."

Did they really have anything to talk about? What made him think she would trust anything he said?

"May I come in?"

She pursed her lips and tried to come up with a reason to say no, besides the fact that he could be dangerous.

"Give me your weapon."

Proud of herself for coming up with that one, she tamped down a grin, squared her shoulders and waited for him to comply. Hey, she hadn't watched all those seasons of *Alias* and *24* for nothing.

He reached beneath his elegant blue jacket and removed a big black weapon. He held it out, butt first, for her. She took it, surprised at how heavy it was.

"You have a backup piece?" *NYPD Blue*.

He reached down and removed another smaller weapon from somewhere near his ankle.

This weapon was lighter.

"Anything else?"

She thought about that a moment. "You have a knife?" She couldn't remember any program off the top of her head with a knife-carrying bad guy.

"No," he said from between clenched teeth.

Testy, testy.

She stepped back for him to come inside. "Have a seat."

After closing and locking the door, not an easy feat with two guns to juggle, she joined him, choosing a seat across from the chair where he lounged. Somehow her grandmother's doilies didn't look at home draped across the back of the chair with him in the picture.

"What do you want, Mr. Blake?"

Despite the lateness of the hour, his pastel blue shirt looked fresh and unwrinkled. The striped tie, a mix of blues and silver, completed the stylish look. Nice.

"I need the details of the conversation you had with Marshall Avery. When and how did he contact you?"

So, at least he hadn't lied about his name.

Alex wondered if Blake took lessons in suppressing his personality or if he simply didn't have one. Then again, guys as handsome as him rarely concentrated on developing their character.

"He called me, asked me to meet with him so that he could warn me about you." She set the two weapons on the sofa next to her.

Blake didn't look impressed or moved in any way. He simply waited for her to continue.

"He told me you killed Detective Henson."

There was the slightest flicker of something in his eyes. Definitely not guilt or remorse, but something.

"Did you kill him?" The irony that two lethal weapons sat on the sofa cushion next to her wasn't lost on her. As much as she wanted her friend's murderer brought to justice she was no vigilante.

"I had no reason to kill Detective Henson."

She would bet a million dollars that the guy could fool a lie detector test with no sweat. His tone was absolutely void of emotion. His expression never changed. He stared at her, unflinching except for that one imperceptible flicker.

How could a man so physically attractive be so cold and unreachable? She never had been able to resist a challenge. In this case that wasn't a good thing. She hadn't needed Avery to tell her that this guy was dangerous. Dating dangerous men was against her own rules.

"Miss Jackson, I'm going to provide you with information that is in direct conflict with my orders." Incredibly his droll, seemingly innocuous monotone was turning her one. "I'm convinced that this is the only way to secure your cooperation."

Her curiosity pushed aside the flicker of attraction. "I'm all ears, Mr. Blake."

"The technology Charlie Crane was testing was stolen from my agency—"

"What agency is that?" she interrupted, deciding that his habit of only hitting the high spots was not going to get them to the heart of the matter.

Another concession to either his mounting frustration or his impatience, his jaw tightened visibly. "The CIA."

Wow. Okay, that was a surprise. Like she would believe that in a gazillion years. "You can prove this?" She made no attempt to keep the skepticism out of her voice.

He pulled his credentials from his interior jacket pocket and passed them to her. There was a snapshot of his handsome mug, as well as all the other identifying information. But IDs could be faked.

"How do I know this is real?" She passed the case back to him. His fingers touched hers at the same instant their gazes locked. There was definite chemistry. The reaction didn't actually surprise her. She knew her weakness for men and he definitely fell into her kryptonite category.

"I guess you'll have to take my word for that."

"Like I was supposed to take Avery's word?"

Blake stared at her a moment before responding.

When he did he spouted off a number. "Call, they'll confirm what I've told you."

"How do I know that's the real CIA's number?" She wasn't going to make this easy for him.

"So call information. Get the number for the D.C. office."

Alex chewed her lip a moment, then went for it. She dialed 411 and selected the option for the requested number.

"Can you put it on speakerphone?"

She nodded and pressed the right button. When the prerecorded voice had completed the CIA's spiel, including the part about their normal business hours, which had passed, the voice asked her to enter her party's extension if she knew it.

She glanced at Blake.

"Three-oh-seven."

A gruff male voice answered. "Weatherly."

"Director, this is Austin Blake."

"Tell me what I want to hear, Blake."

"I don't have the technology in hand just yet, sir, but I'm working on it."

Alex was pretty sure she wasn't supposed to be privy to what the director said next. The man roared about the importance of damage control. The necessity of discretion. And lastly, how time was of the essence. Lots and lots of imaginative adjectives were tossed in for good measure.

"Sir, I have Miss Alexis Jackson here and she needs confirmation that my credentials are legitimate."

The director gave her the information she needed. She supposed she should be impressed, but she wasn't sure about that yet. She thanked him and he informed her of her duty to her country. Nothing she'd heard or seen on this case could be discussed with anyone. She didn't mention the fact that she'd already talked to Shannon, her husband and the Professor. Not to mention Patton, who still didn't believe her.

When the call ended, Blake settled that intense gaze on her once more. "Now, what did Avery tell you?"

"Basically the same thing you just did. Top secret technology, had to get it back, so on and so forth. Well, except the part about you being a killer and very dangerous."

As dumb as it sounded, she really hoped Blake was the good guy. She didn't want to be attracted to a bad guy, especially not a killer.

Blake looked away.

"What's the matter, didn't you catch him?"

Avery'd had at least twenty years on Blake. Surely catching the old guy hadn't been a problem.

"He's dead."

Fear trickled through her all over again. "You killed him?"

Blake shook his head. "He killed himself."

Now we were back to the superspy stuff. "Oh, yeah right, the whole cyanide pill thing, right?"

Intent blue eyes locked with hers. "This is no joking matter."

Damn. He was serious. Avery was dead. "He actually killed himself?" Avery's words about Crane's death not being a suicide filtered through the haze of disturbing thoughts. "He said Crane was murdered. And that there were others testing this technology."

"I think Crane killed himself to send me a message."

Alex shifted slightly, annoyed that the continued hardness in his voice somehow tripped an internal trigger of keen interest in *him* rather than his words, especially considering the subject matter. But there was just something about him. "Why would he want to do that?"

"Because he used to be CIA. I think maybe he realized he couldn't continue to sell out his country and the only way out was death."

Alex straightened, held up her hands for him to wait a minute. "So, he killed himself and just let me find the lens."

"He knew we were looking for him. By killing himself he gave us his position. He knew we'd come and the others would run scared." That intense gaze searched hers a moment before he continued. "It's not as important that I retrieve the technology as it is that I ensure no one else does. Avery won't be the only one looking. He represented an enemy of the United States and that's as much as I can tell you."

"Why don't you tell me what the technology does? Exactly." What the hell could be so important about something that small?

Blake hesitated, but not for long. "It's the transfer link for any computer system it supports. Information, satellites, the Internet, the reach is boundless. A simple implant at the base of the brain and the optic nerve allows full control of the technology."

That was definitely more than she'd wanted to know.

"So all you want is the contact lens, right?" Maybe all she needed to do, now that she'd verified his identity, was turn the evidence over to him.

On one condition; that he see that Henson's killer was brought to justice.

"Actually there's a little more to it than that."

Apprehension worked its way under her skin. "What's a little more?"

"Since Crane and Avery are dead, that leaves me with no way to determine who's running this rogue operation. It's my job to secure the technology and shut down the operation, including all the players. Crane led me here but that's not enough."

If he'd come here to shut down the operation…

"You've been following me." She knew someone had been watching her. She'd felt it on too many occasions lately. "You knew I took the lens and gave it to Henson. You were watching even then. You *wanted* this Avery guy to come after me."

The epiphany hit her so suddenly and with such impact that she lost her breath.

"You've been using me?" she demanded. That was the only conclusion that made sense. "Bait." She said the word at the same time that the full ramifications penetrated her disbelief, allowing her to answer her own question. "I'm the only bait you have left. Henson is dead and O'Neill's in lockup."

His cold, hard relentless eyes stared at her with an

intensity that warned the choice was no longer up to her. "That's very astute of you, Miss Jackson. All I need is the lens and your brief cooperation and we'll finish this unpleasant business."

Alex was tough. She didn't know anyone tougher. She was smart. Damn smart. And no one, absolutely no one, intimidated her. But this guy, she had a feeling he wouldn't stop until he had his way...no matter the cost.

"All right. I'll cooperate. On one condition."

His undivided attention remained on her.

"You see that the local police have the goods on Henson's killer, who I assume is the same one who blew up O'Neill's house, and I'll cooperate all you want me to."

"You're admitting that you have the lens."

Alex smiled. "Let's just say I can guarantee you'll have it...if we have a deal."

"You do understand this will mean I'll be on top of your every move."

Now there was an image she could have done without, considering her current dilemma where this man was concerned.

"As long as Henson's killer gets his, I can do business with the devil himself."

CHAPTER 12

The next morning Alex waltzed into her office to find her entire crew, sans Marg, waiting for her arrival.

"Alex, we want to talk to you."

Alex nodded to Shannon. "Sure." She glanced at Brown then the Professor. "What's up?"

"We've taken a vote," the Professor said.

She tossed her bag onto the counter and then leaned against it. "What kind of vote?"

"We think," Brown said in that saucy Latino accent, "that you have been working too hard."

Alex turned to Shannon. "Did you put them up to this?" She was going to kill her best friend, no matter how nice her husband was.

"It's true, Alex. It's been almost a month since you've even been out on a date. You need a break. Especially considering what you've been through lately."

If she only knew. Blake had sworn her to secrecy last night.

"You," Brown interjected, "need a man, baby."

"What Brown is trying to say," the Professor jumped in, "is that we've arranged for a nice evening for you. A night on the town with a nice man."

Alex couldn't speak for a moment. They set her up on a blind date?

"It's not as bad as it sounds," Shannon urged. "Brown and I put our heads together and came up with a really amazing plan for the evening. You're going to have a great time no matter if you like the guy or not."

Alex opened her mouth to tell them how much she appreciated the thought and just exactly what they could do with it but the phone rang, delaying her delivery.

Shannon's expression went from relaxed to worried as she listened to whatever the caller was saying.

Alex resisted the urge to tap her foot while she waited for her to hang up. She had a thing or two to say to this crew. The very idea that they would think she needed help finding a date was ludicrous. She'd just been busy, that was all.

Shannon hung up. Before Alex could launch into what she had to say, Shannon blurted, "Alex, that was your mom. She sounded extremely upset. She needs you home ASAP."

* * *

Alex tore into her driveway and shoved the gearshift into Park. She was out of the 4Runner and up the steps to her mother's place before she could take a breath.

"What's wrong?"

Her mother stood in the middle of the living room wearing her sexiest red robe. It was past eight, why was she still dressed for bed? Her hair was all mussed and her mascara was smeared.

Alex attempted to catch the breath she'd lost dashing up the stairs. The earthy smell of sex abruptly rushed deep into her lungs.

"What happened?" She told her racing heart to calm. It was only sex. It wasn't as if her mother was having a heart attack. As far as Alex could tell she was stone-cold sober, as well.

Marg shook her head frantically. "I don't know. He…he…we were…" She flung her arms heavenward. "He just made this strange gurgling sound and then he was gone."

Dread spread through Alex, making her stomach roil and her knees weak. "He who?"

Her mother moistened her lips. "Ah…Robert."

"Let me get this straight." The room tilted slightly, but Alex wrestled control of the hysteria attempting to rise. "You're saying that you and Robert were having sex—"

Marg stopped chewing on her finger long enough to interject, "Making love. We were making love."

Alex swallowed just to make sure she still could with her throat contracting with violent spasms. She took another deep breath. "You were making love and he sort of gurgled and then he…" She made a gesture of uncertainty with her arms. "He croaked."

Marg nodded. "I don't know what to do."

Another deep breath. Stay calm. It wasn't as if her mother had murdered someone. Not technically anyway. "Let me take a look."

She crossed the living room-kitchen combination, hesitated at the open door of the one bedroom, then went inside.

Robert, naked as the day he was born, was sprawled across her mother's bed.

"Did you roll him onto his back like that?" It was the most clinical question she could think to ask considering Robert's state. And she wasn't talking about his being dead.

"No…I was…ah…on top."

Alex squeezed her eyes shut to block that picture. "Okay."

"What'll we do?"

There was that little girl voice her mother always used whenever she got into trouble or just screwed up. As far back as Alex could remember it had always been this way. Her mother got into trouble and Alex rescued her. At what point in Alex's childhood had their roles reversed?

She couldn't remember.

"You're sure he's dead?" She felt as if she should be doing something. Checking his pulse. CPR. Something.

Marg nodded. "I tried CPR but it didn't help."

"Did you call 911?"

Her head jerked side to side. "He was dead. There was nothing they could do."

Alex turned and glared at her mother. "How can you be sure there was nothing they could do? For God's sake, Mother, you should have given the poor bastard the benefit of the doubt."

She gestured vaguely. "It's just that…well…he'd already been dead I think for a few minutes before I noticed."

Okay, now Alex was officially scared. "How is that possible?"

One red-clad shoulder moved up, then dropped.

"Like I said, I was on top. I heard him making noises, but I didn't know he was dying. I thought he was groaning. You know, with pleasure."

"You're telling me that the guy was dying and you didn't notice?"

"It's been a long time, Alex," she fairly shouted. "I was going for number four. I was on a roll. All caught up! I don't know!"

Four? The idea that it had been nearly a month since she'd had sex while her mother was getting some nice action abruptly punched Alex in the face.

What were they doing having this discussion? Alex strode over to the bed and touched his carotid pulse. She flinched at the cool feel of his skin. "How long's he been like this?"

Marg plowed her fingers through her hair. "An hour maybe."

Jesus, an hour? Damn straight he was dead. Alex glanced down at his lower anatomy. "Did he take something? I mean…" She gestured toward his erect penis. Too early for rigor mortis. "He's still standing up there pretty damned good for a guy his age."

Marg stared sadly at the well-endowed man. "Viagra."

"We're gonna have to call the cops. It's not like we can put him in his car and drive him home."

Marg grabbed her arm. "Please, Alex, you have to help me keep this quiet. What will it do to my reputation?"

Alex's eyebrows raised. "What reputation is that?"

Her mother huffed indignantly. "Just help me out here. And, as God is my witness, I will never drink or have sex again. You have my word."

Alex glanced back at poor Robert. That vow wouldn't last. But hell, this was her mother. Helping her out was what Alex did.

With that thought, she picked up the phone and called Detective Patton. Man, she missed Henson.

An hour later poor Robert had been taken away in the M.E.'s wagon. The M.E. had told Alex that he suspected a heart attack. Patton had finished taking her mother's statement and gone. Sometime during the whole insane mess, her mother had managed to put on some clothes. Now they sat on her sofa, both too numb to speak.

"I'll miss him."

Alex shifted her gaze to Marg. She supposed it was possible to form a strong attachment in only three dates and one sexual interlude. She'd formed an attachment to Henson in about the same.

"He was really a nice guy," Marg bemoaned.

Alex figured she should say something so she grunted an affirmative.

"Nothing like your father was."

The statement took Alex aback. What did this have to do with her father? He'd been dead for twenty-five years. "I'm not sure I'm following." She cleared her throat and tried to look attentive. Her mother obviously needed to talk and Alex needed to listen.

Marg shook her head. "I know it was hard on you, Alex." She heaved a heavy breath. "But we did love each other, we just weren't good for each other. The jealousy and rage made us do crazy things."

That was certainly true.

She thought back to those days and honestly didn't see how her mother had survived. Maybe the booze had been her only escape. "Dad was a real jerk for taking the easy way out."

"Maybe. I don't know, but one of us had to end it. Maybe he did the right thing." Her gaze connected with her daughter's. "Who knows, we might both be dead if something hadn't given. We were on a fast and furious course toward self-destruction."

That possibility had never occurred to Alex. She'd always considered her father a coward for killing himself when his wife and daughter needed him.

"He knew I would never leave you—" she shrugged "—I couldn't be what he needed me to be and take care of you. So maybe he did us a favor and saved us both by killing himself. We were a lethal combination, Alex. No matter that we loved each other, we couldn't live together or without each other."

That explanation made far too much sense. It seemed so ridiculous to consider her father's suicide a selfless act…but maybe it had been. She'd been a kid at the time, what had she known about love and life and its many complications?

"Whatever his reasons," Marg went on, "I can live with his choice. I married him. It was my mistake. But you"—he stared meaningfully at Alex—"I'm so afraid that the mistakes we made have kept you from living your life to the fullest."

That was just ludicrous. "What're you talking about? My life is great!" And it was. She had every-thing she needed or wanted.

"Alex." Her mother placed a hand on hers. "You can't run away from love forever. Sooner or later it's going to sneak up on you and you need to be ready."

Alex didn't draw her hand away as was her first inclination. She didn't want to hurt her mother's feelings. She was vulnerable right now. This was the way it was with them. Her mother needed her, Alex jumped in and helped. It had been that way for as far back as she could remember.

"Mother, I'm fine. I'm perfectly happy with my life. I'm not interested in long-term."

"You see, that's my point. You should be. And I'm certain it's my fault you haven't let anyone close enough. You've been too busy taking care of me and cleaning up the messes I've made."

Alex shook her head. "Don't be ridiculous. You're blowing this whole thing out of proportion."

"I've depended on you and you've let me, Alex, but I could take care of myself."

Apparently Alex's lack of conviction on that point showed in her eyes. She hadn't meant to let Marg see the doubt but there it was.

"I know you don't believe me," Marg countered. "You think I couldn't get a job. You think I couldn't get a place if I didn't have this one." She lifted her chin in defiance. "Well, you're wrong. I keep the job at Never Happened because I love working with you. I live here because I love living near you. But I could make it on my own. I might fall down now and then but there's nothing wrong with that."

Alex wasn't sure where she was going with all this. "Mom, you don't have to—"

"That's just it, Alex, I do have to," she insisted. "I'm terrified that you don't understand that it's okay to make a mistake. It's okay to fail every so often. Life isn't supposed to be perfect. Living life is about taking risks, about allowing yourself to be vulnerable at times." She squeezed Alex's hand. "That's what you don't get. You *need* to fall. Otherwise you're never going to know just how magical it is."

Her day only got worse.

When she got back to the office, her mother in tow, Brown and the Professor had gone out on an apartment cleanup involving a drug deal gone bad over in Little Havana.

Shannon already had a call waiting for Alex.

Leaving Shannon in charge of her mother, Alex got moving. After the trauma of having Robert die on her and that unsettling mother-daughter conversation, Alex didn't want to risk that her mother would turn to the bottle for solace.

At least there would be no breakup this time.

Alex rolled her eyes. She'd lost it. No doubt.

She parked in the driveway of the house where Walter Brimmer had lived. According to the landlord, he had been one of those obsessive-compulsive people who saved everything. She wanted the place emptied. Brimmer had no next of kin and she needed to get the place cleaned out in time for a new tenant by the first of the month. Mr. Brimmer's attending physician had authorized the funeral home to come pick him up since the man had suffered with severe health problems, high blood pressure and heart problems, not to mention he was eighty. The law allowed for an attending physician to attend to a situation like this, forgoing the autopsy and such.

Donning shoe covers and gloves, Alex took the key she'd picked up from the landlord and opened the door. The less than pleasant odor of molding pizza greeted her. Could have been a lot worse. She shivered as she entered the room and closed the door behind her. The temp of the air-conditioning had to be set at sixty; it was like a fridge in here.

The living room was piled high with magazines and newspapers and dozens upon dozens of pizza boxes. Her nose twitched. That would explain the smell of moldy pepperoni. In one corner of the room stood a tower of aluminum cans. She would see that all recyclables were taken to a center.

Actually, she realized as she surveyed the furniture and what she could see of the floor, the place was pretty clean, the mounds of accumulated stuff notwithstanding.

She moved down the hall to check out the bathroom and bedrooms. The same scenario. Mountains of clothes and detergent boxes and bottles. Tons of stuff.

She'd saved what would likely be the worst for last. The kitchen.

Taking the short hall back to the living room, she wove through the dining room and its boxes upon boxes of cheap china and into the kitchen.

She froze.

Walter Brimmer still sat at the kitchen table.

After squeezing her eyes shut just to make sure she wasn't seeing things, she looked again. Yep, he was still there, slumped over a nearly empty bowl of what appeared to be cereal.

Poor bastard.

She dug out her phone and called the landlord. "Hey, the body's still in the house. I can't touch this place with him still here." The landlord had assured her that the funeral home had been here and gone already.

She listened impatiently as the landlord explained that there had been a mixup and the funeral home was on the way.

Alex shoved her phone back into her pocket and let go a breath of frustration. This was happening altogether too often lately.

Mr. Brimmer dressed well, khaki slacks and a navy polo. His hair had gone gray and thin, leaving his pate bare. He was a little pudgy around the middle. His skin was wrinkled from too many years in the Miami sun. Though he looked a little pale just now since the blood had settled in the lower portion of his body after he'd ceased to breathe.

He'd lived alone. Wife had died years ago. No kids. No close relatives that the landlord knew of. He'd been dead only one night. The UPS guy couldn't get him to the door to sign for a delivery this morning. He and the UPS guy were on a first name basis since Mr. Brimmer ordered so many items from the home shopping network. There was a delivery practically every day.

Alex pulled out a chair and sat down on the opposite end of the table. Rigor mortis had settled in all his muscles, but the worst of what was to come hadn't started yet. She wondered as she studied him, was this how she would end up?

She kicked herself for letting the thought pop into her head. She did this far too often lately. What the hell was wrong with her? Maybe she *was* like her mother and she just needed to get laid. With someone who didn't require Viagra, preferably.

Her mother's words about her not being able to take a chance kept haunting her, making Alex angry all over again. There was absolutely nothing wrong with being strong and independent. Why didn't her mother get that?

Maybe Alex was guilty of not taking chances, but so what? At least she hadn't gotten hurt. She didn't walk around all vulnerable and fragile. She took care of herself.

The memory of Henson's silly laugh and crooked grin poked into her rant, making her second-guess herself. He'd wanted to take that chance with her and she'd walked away. Maybe her mother was right…maybe she would end up all alone if she just kept walking away.

Was that what she wanted? Did she want to never know how it felt to spend years with one man? Did she want to never experience having a child of her own? Just because she wasn't committed to a long-term relationship and didn't have any kids didn't mean she didn't have a life.

Did it?

Was all her bluster really just a way to hide...to run away when she felt threatened emotionally?

Again her mind played a trick on her and an image of Austin Blake filled her head.

What the hell did he have to do with anything?

She was letting *them* get to her. Marg, Shannon, all of them. And all those people who'd died alone...

Disgusted with herself she got up and went over to the fridge. Might as well see what kind of mess needed to be cleaned up in there. Sitting around here having a debate about whether or not she was a coward was getting boring. She opened the door and peeked inside. Not that bad. Milk, cheese, eggs, the usual. Her gaze snagged on the six-pack of Michelob. She looked over at Mr. Brimmer. Hell, he wouldn't mind and it was practically noon.

Before she could talk herself out of it, she grabbed a bottle and went back over to the table. She twisted off the cap and saluted poor old Mr. Brimmer. "Cheers," she muttered, before taking a long, soothing drink.

As if she hadn't berated herself enough, Shannon's thoughts on the matter bobbed to the surface in her head. This was how it ended when you weren't in a committed relationship or when your spouse bought the farm before you. All by yourself. Lonely.

But she wasn't lonely, dammit. Alex cradled the beer in her hands. No way. She was happy. Busy. Even had her own action-adventure subplot going on this week.

Somehow that didn't assuage the sick feeling she got every time she worked a case like this one. Or every time she thought of how her mother really felt about her...did her whole crew think she was a coward? Afraid of life?

She settled her gaze on Mr. Brimmer. Hell, maybe she was. Maybe she'd been running her whole life.

Maybe they were right. Dying was bad enough. But dying alone, that really sucked.

The question was, could she—did she even want to—do anything about it?

Late that evening, after dark, Alex made it home. Her tail was dragging.

The cleanup at the Brimmer location had taken

forever. So much stuff. So many trips to the recycling center.

Despite how exhausted she was, she trudged up to her mother's door and knocked.

When the door opened, Marg looked about as tired as Alex felt.

"You okay?"

Her mother nodded. "A couple of friends from my support group came over and stayed awhile."

Alex nodded. "Good. I'm headed for a shower and a long, long hot bath. Let me know if you need anything."

When she would have turned away, Marg stopped her. "Alex, there's something I need to say."

She faced her mother, had to do a double take to make sure she wasn't seeing things. Marg looked… humble.

"I want you to know that I appreciate the way you're always here for me. You're a good daughter and that means more to me than you can ever know. I shouldn't have said those things to you this morning."

As if that hadn't stunned Alex speechless, then Marg hugged her.

Incredible.

Alex somehow managed to hug her back. "It's okay. Maybe there was some truth to what you said."

Her mother didn't pursue the subject, just kept holding her the way a mother should hold her daughter. Maybe they both had a lot of catching up to do.

A little while later, after her shower, with a Michelob and a brimming hot bubble bath, Alex analyzed the moment. Was her mother finally growing up?

Okay, she couldn't go counting her chickens before they hatched. This was Marg. She could relapse.

But she could also finally move on with her life.

A real life. Maybe a committed relationship.

Something squeezed deep inside Alex. Why did that bother her? She wanted her mother to be happy.

Maybe because that meant she really would be all alone?

Oh hell. Alex set the empty bottle on the floor next to the tub. She had to stop this. This whole poor-me-I'm-going-to-grow-old-alone pity party had gone far enough.

Maybe she would give some thought to this whole "risk" thing. She might even try to stick with the right guy for a while and see what happened.

But that was as far as she was willing to go right now.

She evicted all thought of age and dying and lone-liness from her head and closed her eyes to relax. That second beer had her feeling a bit of a buzz. Might as well enjoy it.

A creak split the silence.

She sat up straight. Drew in a lungful of thick, steamy air.

Another creak.

Wood.

Porch.

Hers.

She was out of the tub and dripping all over the bath mat in three seconds flat. She thrust her arms into her robe and lashed the tie en route to the front door. The house was dark but she knew the way by heart.

Peering through the peephole, she repeated several of the vile curses in her extensive vocabulary.

Blake.

What the hell did he want now?

He'd been tailing her all day. She'd spotted him at every turn, ensuring that he never completely left her thoughts. Then again, that was what he was supposed to do. After all she was his bait.

She jerked the door open. "What do you want?"

"I just wanted to make sure you were okay." He looked past her into the dark house. "Were you in bed already?"

She couldn't answer right away, she was too busy taking in the guy's appearance with the aid of the streetlamp and what little moonlight reached under the canopy of her porch. Suit, tie, the works, just like always. This guy was as uptight as they came. She could just imagine what kind of animal he would be if he let himself go.

What was she thinking?

She gave herself another of those mental kicks. Clearly seeing Robert naked, his penis frozen in erection, had damaged her somehow.

"Are you sleeping outside my house?"

He made no excuses. "Yes."

Well, hell. She stepped back, opened the door wider. "Come on in. I suppose the least I can do is offer you my couch." He was CIA after all, she owed her cooperation to her country, right?

She almost bit off her tongue when her sluggish brain caught up with her runaway mouth. Was she out of her mind?

Yes.

"That's not necessary, Miss Jackson."

She wasn't about to argue with him. "Just lock up when you crash." She'd already opened her mouth once too often today. She pivoted on her bare, damp heel and strode toward the bathroom, only slipping once—from the water sliding down her skin, of course.

Eventually she heard the door close and lock.

By her estimate it had taken Blake a full five minutes to decide to come inside. She'd had time to drain the tub, brush her teeth and climb into bed.

At least there was someone in this world more screwed up than her. He obviously didn't know how to let his hair down. He internalized far too much. All that control had to be costly. It didn't take a shrink to recognize he was unnaturally uptight.

She just wished he wasn't so damned good-looking…and so deliciously sexy….

CHAPTER 13

Alex woke the next morning to the immediate realization that something was wrong.

There was an unfamiliar odor in the air.

There was sound, which she slowly recognized as a television news channel.

She threw back the covers and sat up. The change in position either woke her more fully or prompted her blood to move from her lower anatomy to her brain.

Not only had she awakened to odd goings-on in her home. She'd dreamed about sex. With him.

Hot, wild sex.

She shivered and climbed out of bed.

He was in there. Beyond that door, cooking or something. She wasn't ready for that side of Austin Blake. She wasn't sure she would ever be ready for anything other than the tense control freak she'd come to know him as.

She couldn't exactly hide in her bedroom forever. Glancing back at the tousled sheets, she was pretty sure she needed to get out of this room and clear her head anyway. She dragged herself into the bathroom to wash her face and brush her teeth. A gasp escaped her when she saw her reflection. She'd gone to bed with wet hair. Big mistake. But one that could be rectified with a flatiron and some time.

Thirty minutes later she was presentable in jeans, a tank and one of her trademark belts. She had a thing for belts. All kinds.

She made her bed, just so she wouldn't be reminded when she came home alone tonight of how she'd dreamed of making love with her shadow the night before.

Bad, bad idea.

When she entered the kitchen he was propped against the counter drinking a cup of coffee.

She stopped short of her destination, the coffeemaker. Where was the jacket? The tie? The top three buttons of his shirt were even open.

Blinking furiously, she growled a good-morning and darted around him to get herself a cup of coffee.

"I borrowed bacon and eggs from your mother."

Alex almost spilled the coffee she was pouring.

"You went up to my mother's?" Damn. Now Marg would grill her about him. Letting Blake stay over had been a huge mistake. She hadn't shared their arrangement with any of the crew. She'd known better. They were already trying to set her up on a blind date. Thank God, Robert's abrupt demise had canceled whatever plans they'd made.

"There's fresh orange juice, too. She squeezed it herself."

Her mother? Squeezing orange juice? She didn't even like orange juice.

Okay, clearly Marg had skipped right past the booze and gone for the hard drugs. She was not the squeezing-the-OJ type. And since when did she stock bacon and eggs?

Once Alex got over the initial shock, she had to admit that she was starved. After admitting as much, she couldn't pretend disinterest.

Silently, they prepared their plates and sat. The silence continued, other than the crunching of bacon and scrape of silverware across stoneware.

Alex ate, refusing to consider how this CIA man, this uptight hard-ass could cook like this. She didn't want to know that he could cook. She didn't want to see him without the trappings of his day job. She wanted to button his shirt.

But his lips wouldn't let her.

Her gaze kept drifting down to those nice lips. Whenever he licked them, she had to restrain the need to lick her own hungrily! He was so proper, so controlled, that watching his tongue glide over his bottom lip was incredibly intimate.

She liked his fingers, too. Long, blunt-tipped. His sleeves were rolled up and his forearms were well muscled. He would be really strong. Broad shoulders. Tall.

Her throat felt dry and breathing was difficult. She hadn't had a reaction this strong to a stranger in a very long time.

She stood, unable to bear another second. "I have to get to work." She moved to the sink with her dishes.

Unfortunately he did the same.

Her heart executed a strange little maneuver when she got a whiff of him. How could a guy who'd slept on her couch and cooked a greasy meal smell that good? It just wasn't right.

"You know I'll be right behind you every minute, right?"

She couldn't help herself, she had to look up at

him. He was standing so close…the scent of him…
the pull of his proximity. And those eyes. Intense,
watchful.

"Yeah, I know."

He nodded and for one fleeting instant his gaze
dropped to her lips. Her breath locked in her lungs
and she had to refrain from pressing her palms against
his chest, just to see if his heart was pounding as hard
as hers was.

How could he cast such a spell so quickly…so
seemingly effortlessly?

"Thanks for breakfast." Her voice sounded breath-
less.

"Thank you," he countered, that watchful gaze
studying every feature of her face. "Sleeping on your
sofa was far more comfortable than in my car."

That usually tightly controlled tone was missing
as he spoke…his voice was soft, too deep.

She nodded. "Fine. I should go."

As she made her way to her 4Runner, he tugged
his tie into place and shouldered into his jacket, all
with efficiency and while en route to his supersexy
red Mercedes convertible.

The scene was way too domestic-looking and
entirely sexy.

Not real. Not real. Couldn't be. Couldn't be.

He followed her to work, but lucky for her didn't come inside. Whatever he did with his day didn't matter to her. She just needed him far away. He was the last man on earth she needed to get involved with and she knew it.

"You look grumpy this morning," Shannon said with her usual aplomb.

"I am." Alex didn't pause to say hello to anyone. She went straight to her office, but before she closed the door, she said, "Don't anyone even think about arranging my night for me."

Five minutes later Shannon ventured in to join her. "Okay," she began tentatively, "what's wrong?"

She didn't get too close. Probably because Alex gave her a look that would have made a wartime general wary.

"Nothing." Alex forced her attention back to yesterday's reports. She couldn't remember the last time she'd been working on reports barely a day old.

"Out with it, Alex."

Shannon settled into the chair in front of Alex's desk.

There was no getting rid of her now. Alex could

either tell her the truth or the woman would sit there and harass her all morning.

"Everyone in the whole world besides me is having sex." There. She'd said it. Blake made her want to have sex. With him. Dammit.

Shannon looked a little taken aback. "I know you haven't had a date in—"

"Three weeks and four days." Alex gave her the evil eye. Was she losing it? Had middle age finally caught up with her? Or was she only just realizing that her mother was right and she was a coward afraid to live her life. She was a forty-year-old woman whose life had *never happened*. She shuddered at the thoughts.

How could she feel that way? She'd made a great life for herself. Her business was thriving. Life was good.

Why did who she was have to be measured against the fact that she wasn't part of a pair? And why the hell was it suddenly so important to her?

Maybe her mother was right. The idea scared the hell out of her, but it was possible…wasn't it?

Marriage…kids…talk about terrifying.

But if not those things, then what?

"This is exactly why we tried to set you up yesterday."

Alex snapped from her disturbing thoughts and sent another glower in her direction. "Thanks a lot." Feeling like the fat girl at the prom, Alex tried her best to focus on her work, but her friend just wouldn't go away.

Shannon cleared her throat. "Sorry about your mother's boyfriend."

Alex pointed that death stare at her again, but it didn't stop Shannon from bursting into giggles.

Alex had to laugh. It wasn't funny. Poor Robert was dead. It wasn't funny at all. But still, she laughed harder. Until tears gathered in her eyes. What made these dirty old men think they could load up on Viagra and not suffer the consequences?

"Okay," Shannon said, gathering her composure once more. "How about you let us arrange that nice night out for you—"

Alex sent another lethal glare in her direction.

"You can go by yourself and just relax and enjoy."

Now there was an idea.

She didn't need a man right now.

She just needed to relax.

Dinner went reasonably well. The restaurant was lovely. The food was amazing. And Alex knew she looked great. She'd worn her favorite red dress and matching stilettos. She felt like a million bucks. There were a couple of other tables in the restaurant with only one occupant, so she wasn't the only single diner.

Not a problem. She'd gone out by herself before and managed just fine. The dinner was both relaxing and elegant.

The real problem began when she drove home. Her 4Runner started to jerk as if the engine wanted to die on her. She patted the gas pedal, but that didn't help. The engine ended up stalling just as she managed to ease it over to the curb.

Cursing under her breath, she called for a tow and got out, glancing in both directions. Not so far from home. She could walk it. It wasn't as if she'd be alone. The sidewalk was teeming with Miami's nightlife. Some bad, some good, some outstanding.

She could wait for the tow truck and get a ride home, but she needed to walk. She needed to think.

She strode along the sidewalk toward her side of town. Wolf calls cut through the night air as one car passed. Alex smiled and strutted with all the fervor she could marshal. Might as well enjoy herself. She had a longer walk ahead of her than she'd first thought. The shoes would likely end up swinging from her fingers before it was over, but that was okay. She could use the attention tonight.

The sound of a motor purring smoothly signaled that a car had rolled up behind her. She had wondered when he would show up. She'd known he would be around. Her own personal bodyguard. The question was, who would guard his body from her?

"How about a lift?"

Blake.

Alex pivoted on her precariously high heel. "No thanks. I'm fine."

"I can't let you out of my sight, Miss Jackson."

Damn. He'd most likely witnessed tonight's whole dining alone experience. God, he probably thought she was pathetic.

"Just so you know—" she decided to set him straight "—I don't usually dine alone."

He grinned, the first one she'd seen on those sexy lips. "Don't worry. I get paid to keep secrets. I won't tell anyone you didn't have a date."

She almost slammed the door he'd reached over and opened for her.

"I'm only kidding, Miss Jackson." He looked up at her with those hooded eyes. "Get in. I don't bite."

A ride was a ride, right? She wasn't worried about

him being dangerous anymore. And he had said he was kidding.

Alex climbed into the passenger seat of the swanky Mercedes. "Some car." She sank into the leather interior. It seemed to draw her into an embrace. Very nice.

"My work is dangerous. The way I see it—" he glanced at her as he moved back into traffic "—why not enjoy life? It could end tomorrow." He shrugged. "I live for today."

That was pretty much her motto. Life was short. Live it like you mean it.

"Too bad about your mother's boyfriend."

Did everyone know about her mother's latest tragic relationship? Jesus. Alex was really tired. Too tired. Between the week she'd had and all these emotional revelations, she was beginning to wish she hadn't left the house this week.

"At least he died happy," she murmured. What man didn't want to go with a rock-hard erection?

Despite her best intentions not to, Alex used the ride to her house to study this CIA guy.

He really was handsome.

But he was not the type she got involved with.

She knew better. Letting herself even think along those lines was dumb, dumb, dumb.

"What you see is what you get, Miss Jackson. Nothing more, nothing less."

Her breath caught, but she didn't let his awareness that she was staring keep her from continuing to study that rigid profile. She wondered if he'd meant the statement as a warning or an invitation.

Considering it had been about a month since she'd had sex, dwelling on the idea for any length of time could be a costly mistake.

She decided to find a reason not to be interested.

"You married, Blake?"

"No."

"Ever been married?"

"No."

"Kids?"

"No."

Well, damn. She was beginning to feel as if she'd just walked onto the set of a Capitol One commercial. No, no, no.

"Brothers?"

"No."

Alex pushed a handful of hair behind her ear. "Sisters?"

"No."

If he said no to her next question—

"My parents live in Iowa. I'm an only child and I've never had time to give a long-term relationship the attention it needed."

"So you steer away from commitment?" Interesting. They had something in common.

"Relationships are complicated. I don't need complications in my life."

She faced forward and relaxed farther into the luxurious seat. "I have to agree."

She hadn't really planned to make that confession out loud, but there it was.

Blake pulled into her driveway. He turned to her, the low-slung moon drenching the interior of the car in a soft glow. She wanted to yell at Fate for throwing in one more romantic element.

He leaned in her direction. Only a little. She might not have even noticed if she hadn't been staring at him. In spite of herself her pulse reacted to his nearness.

"The motto I live by is not getting involved with a player. Too much risk."

Alex laughed softly. "Don't flatter yourself, Blake. I invited you to sleep inside my house last night because I felt sorry for you. You're the last man on the planet I'd be interested in being with."

"I don't believe you."

She grabbed the door handle. "Believe what you will."

He was out of the car, coming around to her door and up the walk, arriving at her front door at the same time as she did. She unlocked the door and he went inside to have a look. She tried hard not to let the motivation behind his movements add to her already mounting interest in the guy.

"The house is clear," he informed her as she closed and locked the door behind them.

"See you tomorrow, Blake." She headed for her bedroom.

Long, powerful fingers curled around her wrist. She turned to face him, knowing this was a major mistake.

"Good night."

There was more he wanted to say. She could see the simmering heat in his eyes.

Damn him.

"I'm not having sex with you, Blake."

"I didn't ask you to have sex with me." His gaze didn't leave hers.

"Yes, you did." Saying the words wasn't necessary. She'd seen the want in his eyes.

Now who was in denial.

She eased her arm free of his touch. "Good night, Mr. Blake."

He let her walk away. She would have been home free if she just hadn't looked back.

Some of that fierce control had slipped. He looked almost…vulnerable standing there watching her walk away.

Before she could guess his next move, he was right in front of her and diving both hands into her hair. Her brain betrayed her, left her floundering for an appropriate response.

He tilted her chin up and kissed her.

Not just a quick peck or a smeary smooch, either. He took his time, let the sensations wash over them until her knees felt a little weak.

This was not a good idea.

But it was exactly what she wanted to do.

A mistake. A big mistake.

She drew back. Took a breath. "Make yourself at home in the kitchen if you're hungry."

This time she didn't look back. She didn't even let herself think about what had just happened.

In the sanctuary of her room, she'd just washed off her makeup and dragged on her gown when the telephone rang.

She groaned.

Hopefully her mother hadn't killed anyone else.

She grabbed up the receiver. "Alex Jackson."

"Meet me at the fountain in De Soto Plaza. Ten tomorrow morning. Come alone and bring the contact lens or Detective Henson won't be your only dead friend."

Alex stared at the receiver long after the dial tone had started to buzz across the empty line. *Henson won't be your only dead friend....*

Fear burst in her chest. She dialed Shannon's number. It was late, but she didn't care.

Her relief at hearing Shannon's groggy hello stole her breath.

"Hello? Alex, is that you?"

She nodded then remembered she was on the phone. "You okay?"

"Sure. We're in bed already, is something wrong?"

"No...no. I just wanted to hear your voice."

Before Shannon could interrogate her, she said goodbye and pushed the end button to sever the connection.

She called the Professor next. He was fine. Still up and reading.

Brown's phone rang and rang and rang with no answer. No answer on his cell, either. She left a dozen messages and waited for him to call back…but he didn't.

The fear started to mount all over again.

Blake was right in the other room. He could help her find Brown…but if she told him and her caller found out. *Come alone.* No way would Blake allow her to go alone if he found out.

She would have to go alone. She closed her eyes and prayed that Brown would be okay.

Getting rid of Blake would be the tough part.

CHAPTER 14

Alex spent the entire night worrying about Brown. He never returned her call. While she wasn't entirely sure the man who'd called her last night had Brown, she couldn't take any chances. She had to do exactly as he'd ordered.

"Coffee?"

Alex about jumped out of her skin as she entered the kitchen. Blake stood there, just as he had yesterday, looking not quite put together and with a steaming cup of coffee in his hand.

Why had she ever started letting him sleep on her couch?

The moment her eyes bumped into his, the memory of that one kiss had her pulse reacting. Dumb. Dumb. Dumb.

"Morning." Stepping around him, she poured herself a mug of coffee. She was going to need it.

She had to close her eyes just being this near to

him. Something about him pulled at her, made her want to lean against those broad shoulders.

When this was over, she would get her life back on track. She hadn't gone to the gym a single night this week. Her diet had sucked. She'd barely slept since Henson's accident. And she couldn't keep her mind on business because of the stranger sleeping on her couch.

She wasn't even going to start on the other issues Henson's death and her mother's revelations had raised.

This was not a typical week for her. She never failed to work out. She ate right at least seventy-five percent of the time, and she generally slept like a baby. And she usually enjoyed the men she was attracted to. The difference was, she always steered wide around those in dangerous occupations.

What was wrong with her lately? She knew better than this.

"Gotta get going." She finished off her coffee, grimacing at the burn as it flowed over her tongue and down her throat.

He switched off the coffeemaker. "I guess you'll be riding with me."

Oh damn. She'd forgotten about her SUV. She'd have to call and check on it.

As if riding to work in that fancy car of his wasn't disconcerting enough, this morning her shadow strolled into the offices of Never Happened right behind her. Her blood pressure moved into the stroke zone. How the hell was she supposed to give him the slip if he stayed this close?

Mentally groping for a plan, she headed straight for her office without bothering with formal introductions. Shannon and the Professor stared at her, bemused or befuddled, she couldn't tell, just ignored their questioning looks. "Shannon, I'll need you for a few minutes."

Her friend came into Alex's office and closed the door behind her. "Who's the guy?"

Alex rolled her eyes. "It's Blake. Remember I told you he was following me around?"

Her mouth formed one of those Os of acknowledgement. "He's the guy Marg said was sleeping on your couch."

Did no one respect her privacy? "I haven't had a chance to tell you any of this," Alex said in her defense. Admittedly she and Shannon usually shared most things. "Brown is missing this morning."

Worry drew Shannon's brow into a frown. "What do you mean missing? I just assumed he was at the Ms. Miami registration."

Alex glanced at the door and licked her dry lips. "Last night before I went to bed I got a call from some guy who said if I didn't meet him in DeSoto Park, at the fountain, at ten this morning with the lens, Henson wouldn't be my only dead friend."

"Oh, my God. What're you going to do?"

"Call and delay our first assignment. The Professor and I are going to go in the back and inventory supplies."

"But you did that last week," Shannon argued, confused. "What about Brown? Shouldn't we call the police?"

"I can't call the police, Shannon. It's too risky. Too many things could go wrong. While we're pretending to inventory," she said pointedly, "the Professor and I are going to slip out the side entrance. You keep Blake busy for as long as possible."

Shannon's eyes widened. "But how?"

Alex shoved her cell phone into the back pocket of her jeans. "Just do it. And send the Professor back to give me a hand." She retrieved the tampon holding the lens from her bag and stuffed it into her bra.

A look of sympathy overtook Shannon's expression. "Gosh, all this and on your period, too."

Alex didn't bother explaining.

Once in the privacy of the storeroom, she gave the

Professor the details. Alex listened at the door leading back into the small corridor outside her office. She could hear Shannon talking to Blake. She just hoped her friend could keep him distracted long enough.

She and the Professor slipped out the side entrance. Alex rushed into Patsy's Clip Joint and borrowed the keys to her Bug. She knew Blake would be watching the traffic; they needed a vehicle he wouldn't recognize.

"You're sure you want to do this?" The Professor asked as she eased into traffic, taking a right so she wouldn't have to pass in front of her office. "Blake could probably have helped."

Alex cleared her throat of the fear tightening there. "I can't risk Brown's life like that. The guy said come alone. Even if he figures out you're with me, you won't represent the threat Blake would. This is my fault, Professor, I have to make it right."

"Alexis," the Professor said gently, "in most cases like this, the hostage doesn't survive."

"I know. That's the part that scares me the most."

The drive to Coral Gables had more than tension mounting. Second thoughts piled on. Alex was smart and tough and street savvy but she was no cop or spy. This was not the kind of thing she was familiar with or had any idea how to handle. She'd just have to wing it. Of that, she was not afraid. Of getting Brown killed, she was scared to death.

As she passed Coral Gables City Hall in all its Spanish Renaissance glory, she thought of all the times she'd driven through here, always amazed at the beauty of the thriving community. But today was different. She saw the things she'd always admired, like the exotic Venetian Pool that had once been a coral quarry, and the elegant DeSoto Plaza, but none of it registered as anything other than landmarks leading to her destination.

They were early. She parked Patsy's Bug and she and the Professor got out.

Their first order of business was to find a place for the Professor to hang out while she got into position. Then they talked possible scenarios, none of which had a happy ending.

"Be very careful, Alex," he warned before she left to hang out at the fountain.

At 10:00 a.m., the Professor was in position near the Biltmore Hotel, not far from where Alex was. He'd camouflaged himself amid the gathering crowd of shoppers. Thank God the caller had said ten and not nine. At least now they had the crowd as a cushion for whatever was going down.

She waited by the popular fountain, kept her eyes peeled for anyone looking her way.

At 10:04 a man approached her. Like Avery and Crane, he looked to be about sixty. Distinguished. What was it with all these old guys? Did they have nothing better to do than get into trouble by stealing secret technology and killing her friends?

"You have the lens?"

This one had an accent that sounded British. "Where's my friend?"

"Mr. Brown is waiting in my car just over there." He pointed toward the same parking area where she'd left Patsy's Bug. "When I give the order, he'll be released. Do you have the lens?"

The reality that this man did, indeed, have Brown with him made her knees go weak and her heart skip a beat. She'd told herself over and over that maybe Brown was just out of reach somehow.

She had to stop being afraid. She had to do this.

"You'll never know if I don't see Brown ASAP. He could be dead already for all I know." She said this with all the indifference she could muster.

She tensed as the old guy removed a phone from his jacket pocket and made a call. "Have Mr. Brown stand up outside the car for a moment. If he makes any sudden moves, kill him."

A chill raced along Alex's skin. How the hell had she gotten herself into this mess?

She looked toward the parking area. A rear door on a sedan opened and Brown got out. He looked in Alex's direction. Her heart fluttered with equal measures of fear and anger. A half laugh, half sob caught in her throat. Brown looked as mad as hell. She mouthed the words, I'm sorry.

"Let him go." The guttural sound of her voice startled even her.

The man scoffed. "Do you really think it's going to be that easy?"

She stared straight into his eyes. "Do you really want your lens back?"

"Let me see it and I'll have your friend released."

"You bring him over here, and we'll do an even trade. No tricks."

"You're in no position to make demands, Miss Jackson."

A smile slid across her lips. How dare this bastard think he could hurt a friend right in front of her. "Oh, but you're wrong. I hold the only card that matters to you."

His face set in furious lines, the man made the call. Brown, escorted by another sixty-something man, made the journey to the fountain.

The Professor had warned her that unless the whole business was done out in the open she or Brown or both could end up dead.

"The lens, Miss Jackson." The one in charge held out his hand.

Brown wasn't restrained, but his escort was evidently armed; he kept his right hand in his jacket pocket, obviously ready with a weapon. As furious as Brown looked, he wouldn't be so docile, she was certain, unless he knew he had no other choice.

This was the moment. Her gaze met Brown's and he gave her one of those tapered, cynical looks that said he'd about had enough of these jerks.

"Are we going to stand here all day, or are we going to do this?" he demanded, sounding like a bored Antonio Banderas. "As you know, I have someplace to be."

Damn him. If he made her cry in front of these assholes…

"The lens, Miss Jackson," the number-one asshole demanded.

She reached into her bra and fished out the tampon. "Here you go," she said, passing it to him.

He glared at the tampon, then at her. "Don't play games with me. If you think we won't kill the both of you just because we're in public, you're mistaken. Remember, I'm the one who chose the place."

"I hid the lens inside." She gave him a smart-ass look. "I knew you wouldn't look there when you searched my house."

He started to open the tampon and she tried her level best not to shake. If he didn't let them go after this they were screwed.

"Nobody move!"

Alex's gaze jerked right. Blake? What in the name of God was he doing here?

And he wasn't alone.

The whole fountain was suddenly surrounded by guys in suits just like the one Blake wore. Must be the CIA uniform.

The man who'd escorted Brown to the fountain made a move, but someone warned him to freeze and, thankfully, he obeyed.

The next few minutes were pretty much a blur of activity. Brown's captors were arrested. Blake took charge of the tampon. The Professor admitted that he'd called the office and informed Blake of the situation as soon as he'd gotten into position where Alex wouldn't hear him. The Professor had known she was in over her head. Thank God for his wisdom.

Blake didn't say much, except thank you to Alex

before having her, Brown and the Professor escorted
back to her office for debriefing. Shannon and Marg
had been beside themselves with worry. But all was
well now…they were all safe.

The CIA handled the situation and then they all
disappeared, including Blake. No real explanation of
who the geriatric gang was or why they'd stolen the
technology or where it would go from there. Alex
had overheard something about China and treason.
It was an easy leap from that to the idea that Avery's
people had been selling our technology to China.
The whole thing was over.

Which was, she realized, a good thing. She didn't
need any more trouble in her life and Austin Blake
was definitely trouble.

Saturday evening, Alex, Shannon and Marg cele-
brated with Michelob—wine for Shannon—and
popcorn while they watched a movie. Bobby and the
Professor chose to play a round of chess up at Marg's
place. Shannon hadn't even realized her husband
could play. Alex didn't care as long as they gave the
women some space.

Alex lifted her glass. "Let's toast," she said. "To
Brown." Marg and Shannon echoed her words. "The
best damned Ms. Miami this town has ever seen."
They clinked glasses and drank deeply.

Despite being late for registration, Brown had walked away with the crown. The whole Never Happened staff had been there cheering him on. Who cared if he was a guy? He was one hell of a good-looking broad on that runway. If the judges ever suspected a thing no one knew.

"Alex," Marg said, "is it okay if I use your living room for a meeting of my support group next week?"

Alex resisted the urge to groan. She couldn't believe her mother was sticking with anything. But, hey, she was glad. This was great. "Sure. Just give me advance warning so I can go hang out with Shannon."

"Give me warning, too," Shannon put in. "No offense," she said to Alex, "but I have to make sure Bobby and I don't have plans."

Damn. There was that too-familiar little ache of loneliness. Okay, enough was enough with the whole I-have-no-one-to-worry-about-scheduling-my-life-around crap. Alex was single and she loved it. Sure she got lonely but, dammit, who didn't? Even married people had their lonely moments, when they were fighting or something.

Alex Jackson was perfectly happy just as she was.

She drained her glass and set it aside. Anyone who said differently was full of it.

She did not need a man in her life every minute

of every day to feel complete. She had her home, her business, her friends. 'Nuff said.

She waited for the resounding echo of damn straight but it didn't come. The only thing that popped into her head was the image of Blake.

Just as Henson's death had, Blake's presence had screwed with her perfect balance. Knowing that he'd slept on this very sofa for two nights had her itching to move.

Maybe that wasn't true. She'd been doing some real thinking recently. She could try a mini relationship. See where it went. Maybe she was missing something.

But first she had to find the right man.

Not a problem, she knew plenty. The streets of Miami were full of good-looking, stable men. She'd have her 4Runner back on Monday and maybe she'd just go cruising. Thankfully the mechanical failure had nothing to do with sabotage this time, just a bad fuel injector.

One man in particular strong-armed his way into her thoughts but she kicked him out. He was long gone.

The doorbell chimed and she jumped up. "I'll get it." Any excuse to take her mind off trouble.

Marg and Shannon didn't even appear to notice

she'd moved. They were too engrossed in watching Orlando Bloom.

Alex just shook her head and wandered over to the front door. She knew it wouldn't be Brown; he was parading all over Miami showing off his new tiara. Could be the Professor coming back down for something he claimed he couldn't find at her mother's, like the pepper grinder. Alex had noticed the Professor sneaking a look at Marg at the Ms. Miami contest today. She had the sneaking suspicion the man had a thing for her mother, which could be very good. The Professor would know how to handle Marg's exotic tastes and fragile ego.

Alex opened the front door and all other thoughts, including the one that would have told her to say hello, fled from her brain.

Blake stood on her porch.

"Hey, Alex." When she just stood there, mute, he added, "Can I come in?"

Cheering from the girls at something on the movie nudged Alex out of the trance she'd drifted into. "No!" She stepped out onto the porch and pulled the door closed behind her. "I have company."

A flicker of something in those blue eyes made her chest constrict. Damn this man and his control issues. Damn his power over her. Ten seconds in his presence and already she couldn't catch her breath.

"I stopped by to thank you," he said. "You performed a great service for your country."

She heard what he said, but for the most part she was busy admiring the charcoal suit and silver shirt with the contrasting black tie. The guy knew how to dress. His only concession to imperfection was the way his hair had that just-rolled-out-of-bed look, and even that turned out to be perfect.

She'd pushed the limits of his control that one night when he'd kissed her. She wasn't even sure how it happened. But it had been nice. Too bad it wasn't meant to be.

"Well, I suppose I should be on my way." He took a step back.

Somehow the move jolted her. Wait just one minute, she mused as her attention shifted from how gorgeous he looked to what he was actually saying. There was no way he came to her house on a Saturday night to thank her when he'd already done so yesterday when the lens had been recovered.

"What did you really come here for, Blake?" Her self-confidence roared like a lion. Oh yeah. This guy had a thing for her. Thank God she'd chosen this outfit for tonight. Slim-fitting, low-slung lounge pants and a silk camisole edged in frilly lace. Her bare feet sported sexy pink toenails. She looked good. She knew it and so did he.

He looked puzzled at her question, but he knew exactly what she meant. "I suppose I wanted to ensure that you were all right."

Liar. "You knew I was all right when we said goodbye yesterday."

He nodded.

"So what gives? Did you come back because there was something else you wanted?"

Tension tightened that handsome jaw.

"You want me, Mr. Uptight CIA guy?"

His gaze raked down the length of her body and back. Blatant desire burned there when his eyes met hers once more.

"Yes."

She heaved a wistful sigh. Well, damn. "The problem is," she admitted woefully, "I don't get involved with dangerous men. I've stuck by this rule a really long time, Blake."

Temptation glittered in those blue eyes. "Don't worry, it'll be our secret."

A smile lit her face; she could feel the glow. Now there was an offer she couldn't possibly refuse. Anticipation sent her body temperature soaring.

Oh hell. "But I do have company." Getting rid of them wouldn't be easy.

He inclined his head toward his sexy Mercedes. "The seats recline."

Her smile stretched into a grin. "Perfect."

He took her hand and together they made a mad dash for his car. He sped off into the night, the wind whipping her hair around her shoulders.

She absolutely did not get involved with dangerous men, she reminded herself once more as she turned to admire the driver. But no one had to know. As he said, it would be their secret.

His hand found hers again and he flashed her a smile. Alex knew at that moment that something about this man had forever changed a part of her. She couldn't label what it was…but it felt vaguely like a bond of some sort.

Maybe even commitment…but she would die before she'd tell a soul. At least until she was ready for the world to know what was next for Alex Jackson. After all, this was uncharted territory for her. She wanted to take her time and explore every possibility.

Some things were just too good to rush.

Stability is highly overrated....

Dana Logan's world had always revolved around her children. Now they're all grown up and don't seem to need anything she's able to give them. Struggling to find her new identity, Dana realizes that it's about time for her to get "off her rocker" and begin a new life!

Off Her Rocker

by Jennifer Archer

Available August 2006
TheNextNovel.com

HN53

REQUEST YOUR FREE BOOKS!

2 FREE NOVELS TO INTRODUCE YOU TO OUR BRAND-NEW LINE!

N^eXt ™

There's the life you planned. And there's what comes next.

Life on Long Island can be murder!

Teddi Bayer's life hasn't been what you'd call easy lately. Last year she'd never seen a dead person up close, but this year she discovered one. And it's her first paying client.... But Teddi is about to learn that when life throws you a curveball, there's no better time to take control of your own destiny.

What Goes with Blood Red, Anyway?

by Stevi Mittman

HN54

Available August 2006
TheNextNovel.com

Sometimes you're up…
sometimes you're down.
Good friends always help
each other deal with it.

Mood Swing

by Jane Graves

A story about three women who discover
they have one thing in common—they've
reached the breaking point.

Available July 2006
TheNextNovel.com

When life gets shaky... you've just gotta dance!

Learning to Hula

by Lisa Childs

Available August 2006
TheNextNovel.com

HN55